NO STRINGS ATTACHED

By

Amanda McIntyre

No Strings Attached

Copyright 2016 by Amanda McIntyre
Cover/logo design-Syneca Featherstone
Editing: Kristin Cook
Format: Killion Publishing Services

Published by Amanda McIntyre
http://www.amandamcintyresbooks.com

Manufactured in the United States of America

DEDICATION

To the strong and loyal men and women of the
armed forces at home and abroad. For your services
rendered, your sacrifice for home and country.
With gratitude immeasurable, we will remember.

CHAPTER ONE

"You're out of your mind." Aimee gathered toys and other sundry baby things and stuffed them in her diaper bag.

"Hey, thanks for the vote of confidence," Sally replied, pressing a kiss on her goddaughter Grace Kinnison's tiny forehead. "Gracie would love to have someone to play with when she comes to visit Aunt Sally, wouldn't you, buttercup?" She focused on the child she adored. Never mind her mother, who was her best friend, thought she was nuts.

"Are you hearing yourself?" Aimee tossed her a worried look.

Sally bounced Gracie on her hip. "As a matter of fact, I have been thinking about it—a lot, in fact. Does it sound that unrealistic?"

"Yes." Aimee hiked the diaper bag over her shoulder, and held her hands out to Grace. Grace tucked her head under Sally's chin and pouted at her mother.

"You're not gaining me any points here, kid," Sally said quietly to her goddaughter. She knew that her friend might have a better grip on reality. Maybe she'd grown too desperate to have a family of her own. She'd taken the role of godparent quite seriously, and loved the times when Aimee would drop Gracie off while she ran a few errands. The little girl was an angel to care for with a sweet disposition and bright blue eyes like her mama, and wavy, raven-black hair like her daddy. "I blame you." She placed Grace in Aimee's arms.

"Me?"

Sally chucked the baby under the chin and received a quick, shy smile in return. "If your kid wasn't so cute, I'd have probably ignored the ticking of my biological clock."

Aimee sent her a dubious look. "Somehow, I knew you'd drag me into this." Her expression softened. "Are you sure about this? If you really want a child, there are many out there who need good homes."

Sally nodded. "Believe me, I've thought of that. But when I looked into the process, I discovered that the red tape for a single mom to try to adopt a baby is horrific—even for someone like me who has enough love and means to care for a child. It's an uphill battle."

"But have you thought about the tests, the time off, the cost alone?" Aimee rested her hand on Sally's arm.

"I've been saving and I have the little bit that dad left me.'

Aimee's expression was less than agreeable—more like 'you're crazy' and, possibly, 'you-have-really-gone-over-the-edge.'

Gracie squealed, and her fussing startled her mother back to reality. "We need to talk." She pointed her finger at Sally and used her best teacher voice. "*Before…* you do anything."

Sally found Grace's pacifier in the pocket of the diaper bag and popped it in the little girl's mouth. Her fussing ceased.

"Promise me we'll talk more about this, Sally," Aimee insisted as she jostled open the door.

Sally sighed. "Well, okay, but that means you've ruined my plans to go stand on the corner by Betty's diner tonight."

"That's not funny." Aimee shot her a look of warning.

"Not true. Please, give me some credit." Sally held up her hands. "Everyone knows the Git & Go is the place to pick up guys."

Aimee leveled her an exasperated look.

"I'm kidding. Go on now, your kid is hungry." She shut the door and leaned against it. The house seemed vacant again. There was a silence she no longer enjoyed. Before her friends had gotten married there'd been evenings of impromptu potluck dinners, movies on Friday night with popcorn and wine. But one by one, her friends had found their Mr. Right and were now starting families, starting their own traditions. She was completely happy for them. Family traditions, bonding with each other was vital to the health and well-being of any child. She saw it every day in the students she taught. Those that were nurtured at home, and others left to grow on their own.

She released a sigh, walked to the living room, and plopped down in her oversized reading chair. Drawing the afghan over her legs, she thought about what Aimee had said. God knows she'd dated just about every eligible bachelor in End of the Line under the age of forty-five. A couple had made it to second date status, but thus far *her* Mr. Right had yet to be found.

Sally stared at Rein. "How much did you say it'd cost again?" She'd met with him on Saturday morning at Betty's to discuss the plans she had to remodel her house. It was the first step in her goal of getting her life ready for a child.

Rein sighed and looked again at the floor plan sketches. He'd been the one who'd helped her remodel the family home where she'd spent years caring for her father with multiple sclerosis. It'd been designed to accommodate his needs—wider doors, lower countertops—special touches that allowed him to get around on his own while Sally taught music at End of the Line Elementary School.

"Kitchen, front hall, opening that area between the kitchen and the living room in an open floor concept. And we'll need to get Tyler in there to make sure the wiring and plumbing are up to code. Your old farmhouse is great with all of its woodwork and beveled glass French doors, but they can be a nightmare to do as much as you're wanting to do here."

Sally gnawed on her lip in thought.

"I know that look, Sally. What are you thinking? And if you don't mind me asking, why are you wanting to do this now?"

She glanced up and met his steady gaze. Those crystal blue eyes were hard to ignore. Always had been. That's what had precipitated their short and sweet dating experience what seemed now a hundred years ago. Fortunately, friendship turned out to be a better fit for them than romance. Rein turned out to be the big brother she'd never had and was ecstatic when he and Liberty had married. He'd just announced a few weeks ago, at Thanksgiving, that he was to be a father himself for the first time. Part of her wanted to share her thoughts with him, but she hesitated. After Aimee's reaction, she'd decided to keep her plans to herself. "I've got the money saved to do this."

He shrugged. "I'm sure you do. I don't doubt that you've been meticulous in your thoughts." He glanced at the sketches again. "I'm just curious though—why now? Your dad's been gone now... what is it, four years?"

"Five, this spring." Sally took a sip of her coffee and eyed her partially eaten cinnamon roll—a Betty's Saturday tradition.

Silence prompted her to look up.

Rein raised his brow in question.

"I have my reasons. It's a great old house and I guess maybe I'm ready to make it my own. Anything wrong with that?"

He studied her like he could see what she was thinking. And he was right. She averted her eyes, not wanting to share her reasons yet with the whole town.

"Not at all." His gaze narrowed. "I just want you to realize what you're getting into."

"Thanks. I'm sorry if I seem tense. I have a lot on my plate and I've just been elected to spearhead this year's Montana Buckle Ball. Guess I'm feeling a bit overwhelmed."

"You could say no," Rein offered. "With your house being remodeled, I'm sure the committee would understand."

Sally tossed him a cursory glance. "It seems that my status as a competent woman makes me more qualified than most."

"Meaning?" He gently touched her forearm.

She let out a quiet sigh. "Meaning I have no commitments like a family or children to tie me down."

"Oh, come on now, you don't really believe that's why they elected you. It's because they've seen you pull together that massive wedding for Wyatt and Aimee last spring. That, and how you're damn good at corralling your students."

Rein's smile touched her. "I know, you're right." She toyed with her coffee cup. "It's just…"

"It's just that your girlfriends all happen to be pregnant? Is that it?"

She met his gaze. Sometimes she wished they weren't such good friends. "It's stupid, really." She bit her lip, willing to hold back the emotion welling inside her. "I don't know why it's affecting me so much. It's not as though I'm a spinster. I have plenty of time to find someone, right?" She smiled, though it wobbled a bit.

"You've been so busy taking care of everyone around you, sweetheart, that you haven't had time to think about what you need." Rein caught Betty's eye and motioned for her to bring more coffee.

Sally straightened her shoulders, determined not to let the fear of her ticking biological clock show. "And what exactly do you think I *need*, Mr. Mackenzie?"

"Looks like you two are over here solving the world's problems."

"Just need more coffee, Betty." Rein smiled. Betty had been like a mother in many ways to just about everyone in town. She and the café had the reputation of bringing down-home hospitality and comfort food to their patrons. "And another of your famous cinnamon rolls to go. Liberty can't seem to get enough of them these days." Rein smiled and held up his cup.

Betty smiled as she topped off his coffee. "That girl has enough wiggle room on that body to indulge a little." She winked at Rein then turned to Sally. "Need a warm-up, sweetheart?"

"According to just about everyone I know." She held out her cup, keeping her gaze steady on Rein.

He chuckled with a shrug. "I'm just saying maybe it's time for you to get out and have a little fun. That's all."

Betty fisted her hand to her ample hip, focusing on her task. She slid Rein a glance. "Since when are you giving advice on relationships, Mr. Mackenzie? Seems to me that had it not been for Liberty's persistence, you might not yet be a married man."

Rein held up his hands. "Whoa. Idle down, ladies." He gestured toward Sally. "I simply made the observation that between her job, the volunteer work with the kids from the shelter, and helping with Gracie—"

"That's my goddaughter you're referring to. Tread carefully, cowboy," Sally warned with a half-smile. She knew he meant well, as did Aimee, who had probably confided in Wyatt and soon she'd be reading about her plans in the local paper. She pictured the headline—*Sally desperate for a baby.*

Qualified men needed. Commitment not required, but helpful.

"I'm just suggesting you take some time to think about you for a change."

Sally shrugged. "It's not in my DNA. One of the reasons I'm a teacher."

Betty looked from one to the other, then sighed. "God knows the pickings around here are slim in this little town," she said—more to herself than to anyone else. "Still, Rein has a point. You can't just keep giving. Every once in a while you need to let others give something to you."

Rein ducked his head, hiding a wicked grin. Poor Betty had no idea the implication of her words.

"Shut up." Sally wadded her napkin and tossed it at Rein's head. She looked up, meeting Bettys puzzled look. "May I have a to-go box for the rest of this roll, please?"

Betty adjusted the pen sticking out of her fifties era bouffant hair. "Coming right up." She turned on her heel, the rubber soles of her shoes squeaking on the new hardwood floor put in a year ago by Liberty. Betty had hired her to redecorate, at a time when Rein hadn't yet realized he was falling in love. The man had fought it tooth and nail. But in the end, they both won.

"Hey, what about a double date?" Rein's face brightened, clearly enamored with his great idea.

Sally didn't have the heart to squelch the idea— at least, not to his face. She dropped her chin on her fist. "Yeah, because single guys in this town are a dime a dozen, right?"

"Tyler Janzen."

"Tyler?" She straightened. Rein couldn't seriously think that she and Tyler were even remotely suited for one another.

He leaned his arms on the table, getting into the idea. "Sure, he's a great guy. Sense of humor, and cute, I guess—as guys go." Rein added.

"I hope your wife doesn't hear you say this."

"Hear what? Hi, baby." Liberty leaned down and kissed Rein without apology. "Did you get my cinnamon roll?" She shrugged from her jacket, hanging it on the coat hook on the high-backed bench. Betty's husband had seen them once at a restaurant in the city and thought the cafe should have them. Liberty slid in next to her husband. She wasn't terribly far along—three months, maybe— but with her dancer's physique, Sally wondered if she'd even show very much at term.

"I did. But we can get more if you need them."

Liberty smiled and patted his cheek. "You won't be as charming when you have to start helping me put my shoes on." Liberty turned her attention to Sally. "So I understand you're doing some remodeling?"

"Yes, I am," Sally answered, not wanting to delve back into her reasons why. Instead, she steered away from the topic by bringing up the date-night idea. "Rein thinks a double date might be fun."

Liberty grinned. "I'd be up for that, sure!" Her expression dissolved to one of curiosity. "I didn't know you were seeing someone. Who is it?"

"I'm not seeing anyone," Sally answered flatly.

Liberty slanted a look at Rein. "Are you playing matchmaker?"

"I just thought maybe it'd be fun to do something with Tyler… and Sally."

"Tyler Janzen, the heating and plumbing guy?"

"Rein seems to think he's cute, as guys go. I believe that's what he said." Sally grinned. Paybacks were delicious.

Liberty's brows disappeared into her dark hair. She'd grown it shoulder length and had removed the vivid purple streak from the chopped-off style she'd been wearing when she'd first arrived at the ranch. Her looks then, decidedly Goth, and her edgy demeanor had softened since the arson fire that almost killed her and Aimee and had landed Rein in the hospital with a gunshot wound. It had certainly been a tumultuous year in retrospect, but from the ashes rose a stronger Kinnison clan, and bonds of friendship between the women that Sally felt blessed to know. Liberty's rebel attitude was something Sally had always admired, as it was polar opposite of her practical, common sense side.

"Sweetheart," Liberty said, glancing at Rein with a look of amused concern, "is there something you need to tell me?" A faint smile played on her lips.

Rein stared at her, then snapped his fingers. "Bowling," he said, ignoring her jab. "You like to bowl, right?" He directed his question to Sally.

"If by that you mean, can I gutter-ball, then yes." Sally said. She pointed at Liberty. "Maybe you should ask your wife what she thinks."

Liberty dropped her hand on his shoulder. "Honey, I don't think the doctor wants me lifting any balls heavier than—" She tipped her head and gave him a smile.

"Okay, a movie then." He picked up the drawings and nudged Liberty out of the booth. "I'll be in touch. On both counts," he added, grabbing his coat. He waited, albeit anxiously, as Liberty casually fastened the buttons of her coat.

"I'll just go pay the tab." He scooted off to the register.

Liberty looked at Sally and grinned. "He means well, you know. But, Lord, I love to ruffle his feathers when he goes into bossy mode."

"I know he means well," Sally said. "And honestly, a movie seems benign enough. Maybe he's right, I need to get out and have a little fun."

Liberty glanced up and met Rein's gaze. He was waiting at the front door. "We'll talk soon. But, honey, don't let Rein decide what's fun for you. You make the choice *and* with whomever you please." She leaned down and gave Sally a quick hug. "Are we still on for our girl's potluck next week?"

"Absolutely. I'm going to need your help in planning this Montana Buckle Ball."

Liberty untucked her hair from the collar of the coat. "And when was it you said you had time to date?" She grinned. "I'm there for you. Whatever you need."

Sally boxed the remainder of her leftovers and thought about what Rein had said. A movie might be fun. What she wasn't sure about was going out with Tyler. They'd known each other since the first grade. Quiet, polite, and painfully shy back then, he hadn't changed much. And yes, while he was cute—adorable, really, in a quiet, polite painfully shy sort of way—he was no easier to talk to than he'd ever been. Most everyone she knew felt it difficult to carry on a normal conversation with Tyler. But he and Rein had become fast friends while working on the Last Hope Ranch project and she didn't want to seem unfriendly about the idea. She could handle it for one night.

The bell over the café entrance jingled just before Dalton and his friend, and current cabin resident, Clay Saunders entered. A rush of frigid air swirled around her legs, seeping through her tights. Clay's sullen, steady gaze slammed into her unexpectedly. The air felt suddenly sucked from her lungs. She wasn't afraid of him, not really, just cautious. He seemed larger than life, a layering of mystery and angst that she'd preferred to avoid. It'd been Hank, a common college friend of both Rein and Dalton that had suggested some time at the ranch. A shiver ran across her shoulders and she blamed the winter chill. Dalton spotted her and tossed her a wave as he headed toward the table.

She stood, grabbing her box and coat. "Here, you all can have this booth. I was just leaving."

"Thanks. Hey, I just saw Rein in the parking lot. Said you two talked about the renovations and such."

Squeezed between the two cedars that were Dalton and Clay, Sally set her jaw and prayed that Rein hadn't mentioned anything about the double-date idea.

Dalton raised a brow. "Mentioned that you and Tyler have a hot date."

So much for privacy.

Wedged between Dalton getting out of his coat, the now-crowded tables with the mid-morning rush, and Clay Saunders' mammoth chest, Sally felt her cheeks grow warm. She glanced up at Clay. His expression was unreadable, unchanged. While Tyler was difficult to converse with, Clay was another matter altogether. He was all brawn, honed like a mountain, Grade-A military stock, and carried a lot of anguish from his past. Suffering from Post-traumatic stress disorder, survivor guilt, and missing part of a leg, he was a wounded warrior in more than just a physical sense. He intrigued and frightened her at the same time, especially after the brief incident at the ranch last fall where she'd seen his demeanor change on a dime. Things had been said between them that had never really been resolved. She hugged the to-go box to her chest and tossed him a quick glance. "Mr. Saunders," she offered in brief greeting.

He stepped to the side to let her though the narrow passage. "Sally," he muttered in a barely discernable tone.

"And for the record, Dalton, I am not *dating* anyone." She leveled him an emphatic look, then turned to a surprised Betty standing behind the register. "Rolls were delicious today, Betty." Sally glanced around the small café, aware that the normal chatter had stopped and several eyes were on her.

"Thanks, doll. Don't be a stranger." Betty gave her a wink.

"I still want to hear how it goes," Dalton called to her.

Sally paused at the door. There were times when living in this small town was akin to living in a fishbowl. She caught Dalton's grin and the expectant look of several other patrons. He knew very well that he'd pushed a button.

Dalton was the last of the Kinnison brothers—and the least likely—to find love. But he and Angelique's story had come full circle after years apart and, despite the obstacles they suffered, found love—giving Sally hope that she, too, would find love… just not with Tyler Janzen. Then again, she'd changed her mind about her "perfect man" so many times in the past few years that she wasn't entirely sure she could handle a relationship with any man.

Clay Saunders glanced over his menu, his dark green eyes capturing hers. A snappy comeback to Dalton's remark dissolved in her brain.

Clay took another long swallow of the coffee he'd brought with him. Rein had jostled him out of bed at the crack of dawn, insisting that they had to get chores done early so they could begin demolition today in Sally Andersen's kitchen. He turned as he heard Sally thundering down the stairs and could have placed bets on the fact that she'd not be able to stop when she hit her highly polished hardwood floor.

He peeked around the industrial plastic they'd hung over the kitchen entrance to prevent as much as possible the dust and dirt from getting into the rest of the house. Sure enough, he heard the thud and a gasp, just before a tote somersaulted through the air, its contents of papers fluttering across the floor.

Clearing his throat, he walked idly over to where the pretty redheaded Sally sat looking suitably stunned. He held out his hand to help her stand. "In a hurry?" he said, eyeing those legs in old-fashioned winter tights. She wore a red plaid skirt, decidedly bunched high on her hips at the moment and a black cashmere turtleneck that molded to her body. Her hair was wound up in some twist that he hadn't seen since episodes of Green Acres, but on her it looked damn appealing.

"I forgot I had bus duty this morning." She accepted his hand.

He pulled her to her feet in one quick yank. Her stocking feet slipped a bit as she bent down to pick up the papers littering the floor. "You know they make stair treads and rugs for wood floors." he said, trying to force his gaze not to linger too long on the spot where the skirt curved around her thighs. Bending down was not an easy task with his artificial leg, but he attempted to scoop up as many papers as possible without toppling over.

"Where's Rein?" she asked, not looking up—and, he noted, ignoring his comment.

"Had to go to the hardware store to pick up a couple of things," Clay answered.

"Thank you." She took the papers from him and stuffed them in the bag. Searching around her, she sighed and looked up at him. "Would you mind holding this?" She grabbed her winter boots and, sitting on the bottom step, slipped them over her feet and zipped them up. She quickly slid into her coat. Her hair listed precariously to one side.

Clay fought the urge to reach up and let the fiery waves slide through his fingers. Damn, he couldn't remember the last time he'd even toyed with such thoughts.

"Thank you," she said in a curt tone.

Sensing she was clearly a woman on a mission, he thought it best to step aside. He handed her the bag and did just that. She'd probably bruised her tailbone with the intensity of her landing. But he knew the woman's pride ran deep. He'd bruised it once a few months ago at a moment when she'd challenged him and he snapped, saying some unkind things to her. Things between them had been chilly since, to say the least. He told himself that he didn't care. That she was a strong-willed, bossy, little, thing who could drive a man to drink. But in the dark hours of the night when he was left alone with nothing but his anger and his guilt, he knew that part of what she'd said to him was true.

But he'd be damned if he'd let her think she was right.

He watched her hobble gingerly down the front porch steps to her beat-up old truck. A blue Ford with more rust than paint that was her dad's as he understood. He envied her a little, not only for the truck, but because she possessed something of her past—her family. He had nothing except a sister whose pity had driven him away after he'd come back home and a mother who recently passed from Alzheimer's, never again regaining any recognition of him, but always talking to him about her son in the Army.

"Okay, these bits ought to work better at getting those cabinets out." Rein walked in the back door, his cheeks red from the brisk half-block walk to the hardware store. That, too, had been part of Sally Andersen's past. Her dad had opened the store after moving to End of the Line. He'd thought a number of times of asking Rein about Sally—but the way gossip spread in this little town, he feared that given how things were between them, it would likely only make matters worse. Besides, he had no idea how long he'd stay around. Working at the ranch, helping Michael with the horses, even helping Rein with odd jobs like this wasn't bad—for now. But he didn't want to end up here for the rest of his life. Hell, he'd had plans to go pro in college. He had been the star quarterback. A twinge of a muscle in his thigh caught him off-guard and he gritted his teeth against the sudden pain.

"You okay, man? Do you need to sit down?"

"Stop it."

"Hey, I'd say that to anyone."

Clay held up his hand, holding in the darkness curling inside his brain. Some days, anger was too easy of a response. "It'll pass. I'm getting used to this—he paused— "new leg."

Rein eyed him. "Okay, well, I'm going to get started. I'd like to have the cabinets torn out by evening. With any luck, Tyler will have that new sink he ordered in by day after tomorrow." He stopped and rubbed the back of his neck. "Damn, I forgot to tell Sally we're going to have to shut off her water for a couple of days to reroute the pipes." He sighed. I'll cross that bridge when we come to it. She's got enough on her plate right now."

Not to mention seems a might tightly wrapped. He mentally added, knowing it sounded ironic coming from him.

He worked most of the day carrying the cabinets out to the one-car garage, stacking them neatly as Sally had ordered. She apparently never threw anything away. He stopped to survey the clutter that prevented the woman from actually using her garage. Boxes of old *National Geographic* magazines lined the shelves, along with stacks of yellowed *Readers Digests.* It was a junker's dream. Parts of old lamps hung from the rafters. Dusty old board games were stacked on the shelves, shoved in at all angles. A variety of old tires and hubcaps sat in the corner, teetering like some forgotten sculpture. He spied an old Victrola—seemed in fair condition from what he could see through the thick layer of dust.

"Here's the last of them."

The voice startled him and he turned to find Tyler Janzen. He stood at the garage entry balancing a cabinet in his arms.

"Hey, Tyler." He tossed him a smile as he started to leave. Tyler was the only guy he knew that spoke less than him.

"Sal keeps everything. Says they remind her of moments in her life." Tyler set the wall cabinet atop the others that Rein had brought in. He brushed his hands together, looking around as he spoke, though he hadn't looked to see if Clay had even stayed.

Clay waited politely at the door, his curiosity to hear what Tyler knew about Sally piqued.

"Her dad was the same way. Pack rat. Lord, you should have seen the basement of the hardware store when he sold it." He chuckled.

It was odd that Tyler should be so chatty and especially with him. Since coming to the ranch, Clay had done little to socialize with anyone. He enjoyed the physical labor the ranch offered him. He'd learned a great deal from working with the horses, finding empathy that they'd managed to survive their own brutal nightmares. It'd been enough for Clay. "That so?" he replied, hoping Tyler would go on. He glanced at the man. Nice enough guy, a little on the lanky side, but hard-working and honest from what Clay had noticed. Sally could do worse. He glanced away, slapping himself mentally for thinking he'd have any damn idea about what a woman needed. It'd been well over a year since his fiancée had left him. After that, he'd blocked out all women. Cut himself off for a long time. Convincing himself that he didn't need that kind of intimacy, he didn't think about how good it felt to have a woman curled against him at night. He eyed Tyler and scratched his cheek. Then again—she could do a whole helluva lot better. He slapped that notion right out of his head. "So, I hear you and Sally are going out." It was casual conversation.

Tyler grinned and Clay swore his ears turned bright red, but the light was murky in the garage.

"Saturday night. Just dinner and the movies. Nothing special."

Right. Clay hid a smile. It was clear the poor guy was head over applesauce for Sally. He hadn't quite gotten that the feeling was all that mutual given her response at the diner. And it had been Rein who set the date up, not Tyler instigating it. Clay swiped his hand over his mouth, unsure why that should give him some semblance of satisfaction. "Hey, I'm sure you guys will have a great time."

Tyler, who'd been flipping through an old magazine, looked up as though surprised to still see Clay standing there. "Oh, yeah, it'll be great. I've been wanting to ask Sally out for a long time. Since high school, really."

Clay blinked. The man had to be in his early thirties. "High school?"

Tyler shrugged. "Yeah, I guess with everything going on in her life, I just never found the right time."

Thank God for your friend Rein, Clay thought. "That's a long time to harbor a crush."

Tyler tossed the magazine down. "To tell you the truth, I'm not sure it's such a great idea. But Rein thinks it'll be fun and he said it'd be good for Sally to get out. She's always working, and volunteering for stuff."

Clay nodded. It seemed Tyler, who in the entire time Clay had lived here had never spoken more than three words, had suddenly been struck by a Victrola needle.

"You've dated women, right?" Tyler asked.

He wasn't prepared for the odd question. "Uh, in college. Not too much since I came back home."

Tyler's gaze dropped to Clay's leg. Though covered with his denim jeans and a rugged boot at the end, Clay felt as exposed as if he were stark naked.

"Yeah, sorry, I wasn't thinking." Tyler nodded toward his artificial leg.

"Let's be clear. It's not because the equipment isn't working. I was engaged before I went overseas and when I got home... well, let's just say my fiancée couldn't handle the look of my artificial leg." The truth was it was more than that. His sudden mood swings and sitting in a dark room all day proved too much, and she finally left him. It was easier to blame the leg.

"I've been with women, you know." Tyler cleared his throat. "But no one like Sally."

This was not a conversation Clay wanted to get into. "Uh, hey, Rein is probably waiting for us. Maybe we should, you know, head back inside?" He slapped Tyler on the shoulder, the differences between their experiences... period, like night and day. And his he wouldn't wish on anyone.

Still, he knew exactly what he'd do with a woman like Sally, given the chance while poor Tyler seemed hesitant on the subject. "Tyler, do you want to take Sally out?" he asked, feeling more like a big brother than a complete stranger. Clay could almost see the gears turning in Tyler's head.

He snorted and shrugged. "She's beautiful."

Clay nodded. "She is that."

"And smart. I mean *really* smart."

"She *is* a teacher."

He looked at Clay then, the honest concern in his eyes almost painful. "What do you suppose she'd see in a guy like me? I'm a plumber and a carpenter. I didn't go to college. I was born and raised right here in End of the Line. I've never even been beyond the border of Montana, for God's sake."

Clay understood what feeling helpless was like. He didn't know what in Tyler's past had happened to spawn this lack of confidence. In all other areas of his life, he seemed perfectly competent. Then again, a woman like Sally would be like trying to rein in a wild mustang. She'd been running free, headstrong, and in charge for so long that she'd more than likely run roughshod over Tyler in less time than it took him to change a drain pipe. He had to cut the guy some slack. "Hey, you know women. Just be yourself. You know, do all the right things—open the door, hold her chair, look straight into her eyes when she speaks… it'll be fine."

Tyler chuckled. "Yeah, fine."

"Yeah." Clay nodded and headed back to work as fast as his legs would carry him. He couldn't say why the thought of this impending date kept creeping into head in spite of his efforts to forget about his talk with Tyler. But for the first time in a while, he dreamt of a red-haired woman with gold-flecked eyes.

CHAPTER TWO

Aimee pushed her head into Sally's tiny office tucked into one corner of the choral room. "Hey, are we still on for tonight?"

Had it been a week since her meeting with Rein? She released a sigh. Thank goodness it was Friday. A teacher's ultimate joy. Still, it had slipped her mind that they'd planned a girl's night.

She looked up from the computer screen where she'd been designing a poster for the Buckle Ball. "Hey, can you come take a look at this?" She leaned back in her chair to give Aimee a better view.

Aimee stood behind her and studied the screen. "I like that. Is it me, or did this year just fly by? I can't believe we're already talking about this. Then again, the stores down in Billings are already stocking in Valentine's Day and Easter stuff in the aisles."

Traditionally, Sally ignored the first holiday and quietly spent the second visiting her dad's grave on the hill at the Peaceful Lawns cemetery at the edge of town.

"Hey," Aimee turned to her. "When is this double date? Do we need to reschedule for tonight?"

Sally shook her head. "No, we've postponed it until later. The weather turning cold this week caused some furnaces to go out. Tyler's been working non-stop. I don't even think he's had time to remember to order my sink for my new island."

"I'm sorry." Aimee placed her hand on Sally's shoulder.

Sally looked up at her. "I'm more concerned about the sink, to be honest."

Aimee smiled. "Yep, looks like you need a girl's night."

"I've been working all week on lesson plans and this Buckle Ball. I really could use some help in coming up with candidates for the bachelor auction."

"Great." Aimee patted her shoulder. "Let me text Liberty and Angelique."

"I think the guys are still working on the kitchen, though. Maybe we could start someplace else?"

Aimee was already texting. "No problem. Let's start at Dusty's. I love his Southwest egg rolls and I haven't had a real margarita in months."

"Sounds good. Let me finish here and I need to stop and get gas before I meet you at Dusty's, ok?"

Aimee paused and scanned one of the messages popping up in response. "Perfect. They'll meet us in about forty minutes. I need to call Wyatt and let him know he's on full duty as soon as Rebecca leaves. He knew we might go out tonight, so I think he's invited Rein, Dalton, and Emilee to come over for supper and help. Emilee loves practicing being a big sister using Gracie. And I tell you, for a guy I thought would be a bachelor the rest of his life, Dalton Kinnison is the best father little Emilee could hope for. Ever since he found out Em was his, it's changed him. The three of them make an adorable family and with the baby due in June, I don't think I've ever seen him or Angelique happier."

Sally rested her hand on her chin as she listened, thinking back to all the obstacles the Kinnison family had gone through this past year. "I know, and I can see the change in Emilee in class, as well. Having a mom and dad, with a brother on the way has just made her shine. It's wonderful."

Aimee nodded. Emilee had been in her class over a year ago, and been instrumental in helping Aimee when an accident stranded them at the ranch while on a field trip.

"See you in a bit, then." Sally went back to her task, checking details on the poster design before she printed off a copy to show her friends. It still had to get the chamber's approval, of course, and then they would see to it that it was dispersed in town and within a sixty-mile radius of End of the Line, including Billings. Proceeds from this year's auction were slated for the Billings Women and Children's shelter that Ellie had opened up less than a year ago. Ellie had helped Angelique Greyfeather get out of an abusive relationship back in Chicago and had become even closer when Angelique's ex managed to escape from jail and nearly killed both Ellie and Angelique out of revenge. All turned out well after a precarious time spent in the hospital, but she and Dalton were finally married and had a second child on the way.

Sally finished at school and made a quick stop at the Git & Go to pick up a few items for the weekend. Once home, she didn't want to have to go out again unless absolutely necessary. She admitted to being a bit of a hermit. But she'd grown used to being alone on weekends when others spent time with their families. It had been one of the reasons she volunteered in the summer and fall to give trail rides to the kids at Ellie's shelter. The thought of her last trail ride of the season and the heated confrontation with Clay Saunders reverberated still in her memory. Dirt had been slung, words said that cut deep. Neither had spoken of it since, avoiding the topic by avoiding each other as much as humanly possible.

She dropped a loaf of bread into the basket she carried and was eyeing a jar of salsa when she had the unmistakable feeling of being watched. Glancing up, she noticed Sam Tanner standing directly across from her over the shelf of chips. Sam was the owner of Tanner's Meat Market. He was a widower and handsome in a rugged way, with silver hair streaking once coal-black hair and bright, blue eyes that all but sparkled in his all cowboy face.

"Miss Andersen," he replied, his thick silver mustache lifting with his smile. His gaze held hers as he tipped the brim of the dusty, brown Stetson he wore as he ambled to the register to pay for his groceries.

"Hey… Sam?" Sally said quietly, trying to determine why he seemed to act so strange. He wasn't a stranger. Sally had been going to the market for years and he'd always been friendly, very open.

This bordered on creepy.

She mentally shook her head and told herself that she was imagining things when Sam paused at the door, looked back straight at her and smiled—and yes, it was definitely charming, with a bit of sex tossed in, she was pretty sure.

"See ya around," he tossed out in his whiskey-coated voice.

Her eyes widened in surprise, but her brain couldn't find her tongue to speak. She followed his slow, swagger across the parking lot with her gaze as she walked to the register. "You notice anything odd about Sam just now?" If there were any gossip, any scuttlebutt in town the first to know would be Denise or Betty, and the next would be Maggie, owner of the *Daily End Times* newspaper.

Denise sorted through the handful of change Sally had dumped from her wallet to pay for her bread. She could have used her debit card, but she got a gleeful sense of power when she paid with cash whenever she could.

Denise rang up the item and chuckled. "Hun, you've become about as popular as the Powerball around here."

Sally's heart stilled. "What are you talking about?"

Denise had the courtesy to at least appear surprised. "The buzz around town is that you're looking for a baby daddy."

A wave of nausea assaulted her. She dropped her forehead to the cool, glass countertop. "Please tell me you're joking." She closed her eyes.

"Sweetie, are you okay? Here, maybe you need to take a sip of my energy drink."

Sally felt the nudge to her head and straightened. "Where on earth did you hear this?"

Denise looked at the ceiling as though trying to grapple with the origin of the rumor—which in theory wasn't really a rumor, just a misguided perception. Sally pictured her fingers closing around her once-best friend Aimee's throat.

"I think it was at Betty's." Denise was really pondering this. "Or maybe it was the other night on my bowling league—that would've been Thursday night."

Sally groaned audibly.

Denise studied her. "Goodness, if it's not true, there are certainly going to be some upset bachelors in this town."

Sally glanced at Denise. "What... all eight of them? Nine, if you count the UPS guy who comes through on Monday?"

"Poor guy." Denise sighed. "Kurt, seemed so hopeful, too."

"Oh, my God." Sally held her hand to her forehead, hoping to quell the chaos swirling in her skull. She shouldn't have said a word to anyone. "Denise," she began forcing calm into her voice. "you've got to help me squash this rumor."

Denise straightened her shoulders. "Of course, sweetie. If something isn't true, then for sure Maggie ought not be sending it to print."

Sally's stomach lurched. "She isn't—" She snatched her purse and ran out the door. Stopping to judge the fact that she might not be good behind the wheel in her mental state, she turned on her heel and sprinted down the block to the newspaper office. Checking her watch, she had just enough time to get there if they hadn't closed early for the day. She stumbled to a halt, holding her stomach as she tried to catch her breath. Her gaze zeroed in on the tiny red, white, and blue clock attached to a plastic suction on the door, turned to the side that read 'closed.'

She became a most desperate woman, banging on the door. "Maggie! Maggie!" For a split second she did glance around, grateful that on that particular late Friday afternoon there were few people left, few stores open still. With a sinking feeling, she noted there were no lights on inside the office. She dropped her head against the door, wishing the earth would simply open up and swallow her whole.

"Sally? Sally Andersen, is that you?"

Startled to be recognized, she straightened and saw Nathan Smith, having just locked the door to Smith Drug and Radio Shack, walking toward her.

"Nate. Hey. I was looking for Maggie. I had hoped she'd still be here, it's kind of important. Looks as though that she's closed early." Sally managed a weak smile.

Nathan was engaged to Charlene Whitecomb—a bit of fact that Sally found very comforting at present. Charlene worked in the End of the Line library housed in the basement of the County courthouse in the middle of the town square.

"Maggie was in the store earlier today. Mentioned something about meeting her daughter down in Billings for dinner." He studied her with concern. "Sally, you look a little pale. Can I do something to help you?"

Sally's shoulders slumped. Hope deflated inside her. The upside—if one could find one—is that there was no weekend edition of the *Daily End Times*. The other sliver of hope she clung to was Maggie's professional integrity. Surely, she'd not go to print without first corroborating the facts with Sally first. "No," she glanced at Nathan. "I'm fine." She waved off his concern and adjusted the collar of her coat around her neck, realizing then she'd left her gloves and hat in the truck back at the store. "It's been a dreadfully long week—for you, too, I'm sure. Nothing one of Dusty's famous margaritas won't cure."

Nate's gaze cut across the street where Charlene was walking across the courthouse lawn to meet him.

"You two have big plans tonight?" Sally asked, grateful to turn her thoughts—and Nate's—elsewhere.

"We're going to catch dinner at Betty's, and then hit a movie tonight." He smiled, unable to take his eyes off the petite blonde who returned his smile, her face beaming.

Sally was happy for them, truly. It's just being this close to her least favorite holiday was tainting her generosity… that, and recent events. Valentine's Day for her had become the day she ordered in pizza, coupled with her favorite wine, shut the blinds and read all day in her pajamas. "Sounds lovely. Have a great evening." She started to walk away, and was surprised when Nate grabbed her arm.

"Sally," he said lowering his voice as she took a step closer. "I'm only a pharmacist, but if I might offer some advice?"

Sally eyed his grasp and detected he was completely serious. "Sure, Nate, what is it?"

He cleared his throat. "It's just that too much alcohol can cause issues... especially if, you know...."

"Know?" Sally prompted, having no idea where Nate was going with this strange conversation.

"If you're trying to get pregnant," he whispered leaning down toward her ear.

Sally withdrew her arm from his grasp. Maybe he was joking. She waited for him to laugh—tell her he meant nothing by it.

He didn't.

"Does everyone in town know about my life?" she asked. She suddenly felt as though she were the lead in a sitcom gone horribly wrong.

Nate gave her a brotherly smile. "Just watching out for our own, right?"

Sally nodded. Could this nightmare get any worse?

Nate patted her arm, and in the next moment, reached out to take Charlene's hand.

"Hi, Sally," Charlene bubbled forth in a bright, I-have-no-problems-in-the-world voice.

Sally bit back a sob, and made a beeline for her truck.

A few moments later, she sat behind the wheel in Dusty's parking lot. Already several patrons were gathered there, given the number of vehicles in the lot. She gripped the wheel and told herself she should just go home, put a quarantine sign on her door, and call in sick for the next...oh, maybe the next five to ten years. Long enough for people to forget.

She knew better. Hell, people still talked about Nate's grandfather, a decorated WWII veteran, who one Friday night decided to streak across the football field during the halftime band performance in solidarity of his peer's request for a nude beach day as part of the resident activities at the Sunnyside Nursing Home.

George Smith was apprehended and eventually set free on bond. A couple of band members quit the band. The nursing home allowed George to stay, but nude beach day never happened. Still, it didn't stop folks from reminiscing now and then, just for a good laugh.

Sally figured she didn't have a prayer of people forgetting this rumor anytime soon. She noted Aimee's SUV and Liberty's truck and knew her friends were inside waiting for her. Taking a deep breath, she grabbed her keys and bag, and walked in to face the proverbial music, with her head held high.

Rein glanced at Clay. "You're sure you don't want to come on back to the ranch? Wyatt's making his famous chili, and if Gracie behaves, we might get in a game of poker."

Clay watched his friend load the last of his tools in the lockbox in the back of the truck. He reached inside the cab of his truck and slipped a relatively clean sweatshirt over the shirt he'd been working in all day. He'd gotten used to the altitude of the mountains finally, far removed from his Texas roots or even California, where he'd lived for a short time with his sister. But the air had turned colder as the sun started to set—colder as in the Polar Vortex variety. "Might join you later. I told Tyler I'd meet him for a beer over at Dusty's."

Rein grinned as he yanked open the driver's-side door. "Be careful. I hear the girls are meeting there tonight to discuss this year's bachelor auction."

Clay frowned. He hadn't lived in this area for too long, and frankly, he didn't know how much longer he'd stick around. But being single, his interest was piqued. "What's that all about?"

Rein shrugged into his Carhartt jacket. "Every spring the town's Chamber puts on what they call the Montana Buckle Ball. It's normally held at the high school gym. I went one year, but Wyatt and Dalton could never be convinced."

"Convinced... of what?" Clay flipped through his wallet to check his finances for the evening.

"To take part in the bachelor auction. They get five or so single guys in town, dress them up, and auction them off to the highest bidder for a date."

Clay glanced up. *Was he serious?*

Rein continued, "The proceeds from the bids go toward charity. One year it was the End of the Line fire department; another it was the Billings Children's Hospital. I heard they were talking about the recipient being the Billings Women's and Children's Shelter that Ellie just opened this past year. Heard she was already running out of room in that big old house we helped her with. That lady does some amazing work down there."

While Clay agreed, and he'd happily offer a donation to Ellie for her shelter, he knew how to say no. "Thanks for the two-minute warning. Might be a good idea for Tyler, though. Seems like he's kind of ready to settle down."

Rein scratched the back of his neck. "Yeah, I tried to find a way to hook him up with Sally."

Clay nodded. "Yeah, I heard something about that."

"You did?" Rein asked.

"Pretty much the whole town knows, bro." Clay smiled. Did the guy really not get how fast news like that can travel in a small town? "Sally didn't seem too keen on the idea when Dalton asked her about it."

His friend sighed. "Yeah. I've known Sally a long time. She and I tried dating once or twice."

"And?" Why this bit of information should interest him, he didn't know, but it did.

"Didn't really work out. We decided we were better off as friends," Rein answered.

His reply dredged up a few questions in Clay's mind, but he thought it best to let them slide. "Well, listen, I better head out. See you later?"

Clay wasn't thrilled about the idea of being in a crowded room of potentially drunk folks tonight. Most of his weekend nights had been spent down in his cabin, parked on his couch watching old movies or practicing his shooting skills in Call of Duty. Still, Tyler had asked him and so he stuffed his keys in his pocket and sauntered up to the door.

Despite the no-smoking sign on the door, it was clear that at one time it'd been allowed. The musty odor of stale smoke seemed infused in the rough-hewn floors, and walls. Clay had come up to Dusty's a couple of times with Dalton. He liked

Dusty. Seemed like a nice guy. Treated everyone the same.

"Hey, Clay, good to see you. The place is pretty full tonight." Dusty leaned against the end of the bar, talking to Clay as though he was the only guy in the place. "If you're looking for Dalton, I haven't seen him."

Clay scanned the room, and while he told himself he was looking for Tyler, he knew that was a lie. His gaze landed on Sally Andersen seated in a booth at the end of the room. She was with Liberty, Aimee, and Angelique and a young woman who'd pulled up a chair at the end.

Not that he cared. His gaze zeroed in on that insanely red hair she had wrapped up in some clip, a few corkscrew tendrils falling gently around her face. Travesty for hair like that to be held prisoner in a hair clip. She glanced over. He was pleased when her eyes met his. He felt a sucker punch to his gut and forced a quick smile.

"Clay!"

He glanced with half-interest toward where he'd heard his name being called. There was Tyler, hand raised, waving him to a table. He checked only once as he wove through the crowded tables to see if Sally was watching, but she'd gone back to her friends.

"Hey, glad you could make it. I was about to order." Tyler caught the attention of a waitress.

"Good evening, gentlemen. My name is Dixie, and I'll be serving you tonight." She looked at both men, and her gaze lingered on Clay. "What can I get you, cowboy?"

"You have any specials tonight?" Clay asked, avoiding how the woman was eyeing him.

"Dusty's burger is on special. Comes with one side. Draws are only two dollars if you order the burger."

"Sounds good," Tyler answered. "Bring me a Guinness stout."

"I'll have the same," Clay responded, handing Dixie the menu.

She took both menus and smiled at Clay as she left.

Tyler, looking a tad nervous, leaned forward. "Hey, did you hear about Sally?"

Lately, she seemed to be popping up in his life. Even so, he'd never been much for small town gossip. He'd grown up in a sleepy little town down in Texas, the kind of place where you never locked your doors. Which is how his dad had been found sleeping with one of the waitresses of the Dairy Sweet—when her husband came home early from his night shift at work. That pretty much changed his life. He and his sister wound up in a trailer court outside of town. She used to clean people's houses for a living, take in ironing. He'd hated it. "Nope." He scanned the room, hoping that Tyler would sense his disinterest.

"Rumor has it that she's looking for a baby daddy."

What the fuck? He had to hold back from grabbing Tyler by his plaid snap shirt. "Man, did you just hear yourself?"

Tyler put his hands up in defense. "Hey, I didn't start it."

"I thought Sally was your friend," Clay challenged him with a pointed look.

"Well, she is." Tyler appeared to get the idea he might have been talking too loud. He leaned forward, lowering his voice. "If Sally wants a baby, that's cool. I understand she just doesn't want a husband to go with it."

Clays gut clenched. "You know that doesn't sound like Sally. Come on. I hope you're not perpetuating this kind of crap, because that's what it is, crap." Clay looked over at Sally and watched as she listened attentively to Aimee explaining something. Yeah, she was too smart to even think of such a thing. Not having a dad, even as old as he was, was a bitch.

"You're the only one I've said anything to about it. Thought maybe she might have mentioned something to you, is all." Tyler looked up and beamed at Dixie as she placed their food and drinks on the table.

"You boys let me know if you'll be needing anything else." Dixie offered Clay a wink. Tyler had already dived into his food.

"Where'd you hear this?" Clay asked after taking a healthy drink of his beer.

"Over at Betty's the other day—at breakfast with some of the guys in town." Tyler took a minute to chew his food and swallow. "We were talking about the Buckle Ball and how Sally's in charge of that this year."

"Yeah, I heard something about a bachelor auction," Clay remarked.

Tyler nodded. "Exactly. Then Sam says that Wyatt came in the other day and sort of let it slip that she was thinking of starting a family."

"That doesn't mean a thing. Women talk about that stuff all the time."

Tyler tilted his head. "True, but Wyatt said that Aimee was concerned because Sally had mentioned using unconventional methods."

Clay chuckled. "Last time I checked having sex was kind of the conventional method."

"If you're not smart, or if you want a kid bad enough. But there was nothing said about being interested in anyone—you know, in a romantic way."

"Maybe she's going the artificial route," Clay offered as a way to detour his mind from imagining Sally in a tangle of sheets, her red hair spilling over the pillows.

Tyler took another bite of his burger and seemed to ponder that. "Possibly. But that costs a lot of money, and with all the stuff she's doing on the house, seems a bit improbable."

Clay wasn't sure how to respond. It wasn't his business.

"Hey, I'm going to go over and say hi. You want to come?" Tyler was halfway out of his chair.

"Nah, you go on. I'm good."

Clay dug into his meal, trying to ignore how it bothered him that Tyler had slid into the booth next to Sally after Aimee excused herself to make a call. He chided himself that it was the only seat available. But he found himself thinking about what Tyler had said and the way Tyler's shyness around Sally had seemed to suddenly disappear. Clays gaze was steady on Tyler as he casually dropped his arm over the back of the booth behind Sally's shoulders. The cute blonde, seated in the chair at the end, seemed quite focused on Tyler. But what the hell did he know about the women around here... about women, period. He'd *thought* he knew the woman he was once engaged to... three weeks after he arrived stateside, the Army flew her out to Boston where he was recuperating. He hadn't gotten his new leg yet. One look at that and she was history. She mailed the ring to him a week later.

He shook his head to dispel the memory. He had no business traveling down that road again. He finished his beer and was debating a second burger when Tyler returned.

"Just thought I'd be neighborly." Tyler settled in his chair.

"You want another beer? I'm buying."

"Sure," Tyler said with a shrug.

Sally, and her entourage met Aimee at the front of the bar. They paid their tab and left. Clay breathed a little easier.

"That blonde, did you see her? She's Angelique's new assistant over at the satellite clinic. Her name is Kaylee."

Dixie stopped at the table. "You boys need anything?"

"Two more beers and another burger." Clay said. "You want another?" He pointed to his dinner partner.

"Just the beer. I'm good." Tyler had barely started his meal when he went to flirt with Sally.

"So, this Kaylee? Is she around for a while?" Yeah, he was baiting the poor guy.

Tyler looked up in surprise. "Yeah, she's moved into an apartment over Betty's diner. Temporary, until she can find a place."

Tyler stuffed a fry in his mouth and eyed Clay. "Why do you ask?"

Man code for: *hands-off*. Clay smiled. At least his focus wasn't on Sally. That somehow made Clay feel better. Not that he was interested. Yeah, that was a load. She was a good-looking woman, no doubt. And after the things they'd said to each other last fall, he was pretty sure that he had no chance in hell coming within ten feet of Sally Andersen unless it was to work on her house.

He happened to look over just as Sally dropped her wallet in her purse. She looked up and he let his gaze linger a little longer than necessary. She blinked, ducked her head, and hurried out the door.

"She sure is hot."

Clay's attention snapped back to Tyler's. He was about to take another bite of his burger. "Who is?"

Tyler frowned. "Kaylee, of course."

Clay was grateful when Dixie brought his beer and more food to occupy the thoughts running through his head.

He left the bar after Tyler wanted to play a round of pool with some guys from north of town. He nearly skated his way to the truck. The snow was coming down fast and heavy, and had quickly blanketed the parking lot and the streets. He made a quick stop to fill his truck and pick up a few groceries for the weekend. There were a couple of good wild card games on this weekend that he wanted to see.

He picked up some cornbread mix, some soup starter, fresh veggies, and some chicken breasts, his mouth watering at the scent of his mom's recipe of chicken soup cooking on the stove. On a day like today, that soup meant he was home, where it was safe and warm. Julie, his older sister, hadn't transitioned to life in the trailer very well. She chose to be gone as much as possible, it seemed. Clay would watch his mom cook amazing comfort food dishes with what they had. He'd even helped her plant a small garden along the edge of the trailer home. Clay grew large and strong, excelling in nearly every sport throughout his school career. He attended college on academic and sports scholarships, but never lost his love for cooking, and it came in handy on game days when he'd cook for the team, impressing his teammates with his down-home culinary skills.

He carried three bags to the truck, slipping and sliding on the walkway. The heavy, wet snow would have been difficult on two good legs, much less on a newly designed metal leg he was still getting used to. He had to scrape a thick coating of ice from his windshield that had formed in the short time he was in the store. It made him realize that no snowplow was going to venture out in this, and he sure as hell wasn't interested in taking on the treacherous mountain roads at this hour. He peered across the lot, seeing icy sheets of snow slicing at a hard angle in the streetlight. He couldn't see the bowling alley across the street. Climbing into his truck, he decided to give Tyler a call and ask if he could crash on his couch for the night. He let it ring several times and finally made the decision to drive the few blocks there. As he drove out of the lot, he could barely discern where the main road was and he hoped that Aimee and the girls had all decided to get home before this mess hit. He slid to a four-way stop and as he waited, dialed Rein.

"Hey, Clay. Where are you?" Rein asked.

"Still in town. Think I'm going to head over to Tyler's place and crash there." He looked through his windshield, waiting on the light to change. "I was calling to see if Aimee and the girls got home safely."

"They called earlier and we told them to stay in town. They're all over at Sally's. Yeah, best you stay in town—you don't want to get out on that mountain road in this shit."

"Okay, I'll meet you over at Sally's in the morning." The light turned green and Clay crept forward. He couldn't remember a time when he'd seen it snowing so hard. "That is, if you can get in."

"I'll call you," Rein stated. "Hey, can you do me a favor and maybe run by Sally's, make sure the electricity is working? Our lights out here have flickered a time or two, but Wyatt's got the generator."

"I can do that. I'm not too far from there."

"Thanks, appreciate that. A little nervous with two pregnant women out there."

"I'm sure Sally has them all quite comfortable."

"I'm sure she does," Rein responded. "Oh, and Clay. you might not want to let on that you're there on a checkup mission. You're walking into a house of alpha women, bro."

Clay smiled. He'd fought alongside some of the finest women on the planet. He could handle it. "I'll use the excuse that I stopped by to pick up my tool belt."

"Hey, that'll work," Rein agreed.

Clay hung up and shook his head. "Yeah, in the middle of some damn snowstorm. Not too transparent.

CHAPTER THREE

"Well, it certainly seemed Tyler was receptive to the idea of helping us out with the bachelor auction." Liberty sat on the rug in front of Sally's fireplace, roasting a marshmallow.

Sally sat with her legs curled under her at one end of the sagging, old camelback Victorian couch, she'd found at an estate sale one frivolous weekend. Aimee sat at the other end, wrapped in one of the many afghans Sally kept in the front sitting room. Replacing all the windows in her house was yet another thing on her to-do list which seemed to grow every time she sat for more than three seconds alone in her house.

"He did, but you have to remember Tyler is a one of our returning bachelors this year," Angelique offered, sipping the orange juice and ginger ale drink that Sally had made for the non-wine drinkers in the group.

Sally had to admit that the impromptu sleepover made possible by the worsening weather conditions had served to brighten her spirits. She and Aimee had spoken privately earlier in the evening and her friend had offered her apologies more than once.

"I told Wyatt that you'd decided to pursue a child of your own. He was feeding Gracie. I was in the kitchen. His response was 'that's nice.' And that it was it. He must have mentioned it to Rein, but I have no idea how it got started around town."

Sally didn't blame Aimee. News like this doesn't stay sedentary, once revealed, for very long. It's as though it takes a life of its own. She had shrugged and found herself easing Aimee's torment with having told Wyatt. "Chances are it will die out when the next 'big' thing comes along." And she made the decision to put the strange day behind her.

The wind outside whistled around the corner of the house, making Sally glad to be nestled inside with her best friends. "Okay, ladies, help me make a list of potential candidates for the auction."

"Sam Tanner?" Liberty suggested. "He's single, well—a widower, right? But the guy could be Sam Elliot's stunt double." She smiled, then seemed to ponder. "But I bet he does his own stunts." She popped a charred marshmallow in her mouth.

"There is Evan Littlefield, Jr. Didn't he just come back to work with his dad over at Montana West Bank?" Angelique piped up.

Sally added the name to her list. Evan was not necessarily her *cuppa*, though a nice man, so she understood… mostly from Betty. Mentally, she chided herself for being as much a part of a paying passenger on the gossip railway in this town as a victim of it. "Who else? We have Tyler on board."

"Oh, how about Reverend Bishop from church?" Aimee offered. The Kinnison clan and a few friends had had a private baptism ceremony for Grace a few months back one Sunday after church. It'd had been the Reverend Adam Bishop's first baptism since taking over the First Church of Christ from the retiring Pastor Riggs. "He seems like a nice man and he'd certainly be on board to help Ellie and the shelter out if he could."

"I saw him at the store the other day," Angelique remarked. "He's kinda cute… in a very clean-cut sort of way."

"Polar opposite of Dalton, you mean." Liberty interjected with a grin.

Angelique shrugged. "Always had a soft spot for bad boys, I guess."

"Well, Dalton can try all he wants to give off the bad boy vibe, but deep down he's a total family guy. You can see that with how he is with Emilee," Liberty said.

Angelique smiled and gently rubbed her hand over her swollen belly. "We're all very excited about adding another one to our family." She and Dalton had only just reconnected after years of separation after a single night of unbridled passion left Angelique pregnant with Emilee. Last year, Angelique's husband escaped jail and in a fit of revenge found and attacked Angelique where she'd been assisting at a veterinarian clinic in Billings. She survived and, by some miracle so had her and Dalton's unborn baby. She hadn't known she was pregnant when attacked. Dalton had wasted no time after Angelique recovered in getting married at the courthouse and making sure his name appeared officially on Emilee's birth certificate.

"Is it a boy?" Aimee asked.

"That's what the radiologist indicated with my ultrasound the other day." Angelique smiled.

"Emilee called it. I'm starting to wonder if she really does have her great-grandmother's gift of being a seer."

"Dalton must be over the moon," Sally said. She was so happy things had turned out as they had. Given the circumstances, it could have been much worse.

"Oh yeah, and you should see him and Emilee planning out the nursery." She grinned as though picturing them in her mind. "Emilee is very emphatic about what colors her brother is going to like. Dalton's not really fighting her on any of it."

"The girl does have some kind of gift, that much is true." Liberty shook her head. "That could get interesting in the teen years, mama."

Angelique nodded. "Don't think I haven't thought about that."

"Oh, what about Justin Reed?" Aimee said.

"Who's that?" Kaylee straightened in her chair. It was clear that Kaylee would soon be saving her pennies for this auction.

"Sure, the new history teacher who replaced Mr. Worth after his heart attack. Great idea! He's twenty-seven, unattached, and just moved here." Sally made some more notes on her yellow legal pad.

"So, as long as we're on the subject of eligible bachelors, can we talk about Tyler for a minute?" Liberty shifted so she could face Sally.

"What about him?" Sally shrugged.

"Well, tonight over at Dusty's was clearly some advanced flirting if I ever saw it."

Sally shook her head. "That's just Tyler. He's a different guy in private, trust me," Sally said, and went on with making notes.

Aimee looked from one woman to the other. "Did I miss something when I went to call Wyatt?"

"Just Tyler making moves on our Sally," Liberty interjected.

"No moves were being made." Sally batted away the implication.

"He's a really sweet guy," Angelique offered.

"I think he's hot," Kaylee stated, and then, realizing she'd spoken aloud covered her mouth. "I think maybe I've had too much wine."

Sally smiled, then looked at Liberty. "He is a sweet guy. I've known him practically my whole life. He's like a brother to me."

"I'd say we better fill Rein in on that since he thinks the two of you would be great together."

"Yeah, and when did someone make him town matchmaker, anyway?" Sally piped up.

"Okay, if not Tyler, then we need to find you another guy." Liberty stood and looked around. "Where's your laptop?"

"On my desk, over there...why?" Sally followed as Liberty made a beeline to her computer. "What are you doing?"

"Well, I happened across this the other day," she glanced at Sally, "after Rein started trying to be matchmaker. I figured it might be a safer approach."

"To what?" Sally asked.

"To finding you a cowboy to ride you off into the sunset, of course." Liberty waggled her dark brows. "All we have to do is set up your profile on Montana.Match.com."

The wine Sally had taken a sip of spewed from her mouth. "You're what? No. No. No. I don't think so. What makes you think I'm interested in dating?" Sally went to the kitchen for a towel and some vinegar to clean the splatters of wine off her wool rug.

"You're not?" Angelique asked. "But I thought…."

Sally, on all fours, dabbed at the spots. Her week came out in her fervor to remove the stains—Sam's odd looks, Denise's revelation, Nate's cautioning her on what not to drink—had about caused her to snap. "What I mean is—" She ground the cloth into the stain. "Even if I had time to date, which I don't, I don't want to expose myself to a bunch of strange men on the Internet just to find Mr. Right."

"And Tyler?" Aimee asked.

Sally tossed her a look. "Mr. Right for someone else."

Kaylee clapped her hands in glee and realized everyone was staring at her. "Sorry."

Liberty grinned. "Well, love, I'm pretty sure they require you to be fully clothed in your profile picture." She offered Sally a wicked grin.

All eyes and a couple of groans landed on Liberty.

The lights flickered and then the house went dark, with the exception of the diminishing fire in the fireplace.

"Guess that answers that question." Liberty returned the laptop to the desk.

"I'll go get a couple more logs," Kaylee said, jumping up.

Sally rummaged through her desk drawer, found a box of matches, and began to light the variety of candles she had lined up on the mantel. Most hadn't been lit since she bought them, causing the flames to snap from the dust until the heat dissolved it.

"Kaylee seems nice," Sally said, glancing down at Angelique as she lit the last votive.

"She is very good with the animals at the clinic, but I think she misses living in the city where there's more things to choose to do on a Friday night."

"Seems she may have already found something that could keep her nights busy." Liberty smiled as she drew the afghan around her shoulders and parked herself on the couch between Aimee and Sally.

Kaylee returned, arms laden with a stack of logs that she dumped in the basket. She went about the task of building the fire back to blazing, the heat reaching out into the room.

"So," Liberty said, capturing Sally's gaze. "Why don't you give us your criteria, Ms. Andersen."

Sally had finished refilling her guest's drinks and settled in beside her friend. "What do you mean, criteria?"

Liberty shrugged, glanced at Aimee and Angelique, then back at Sally. "We've all heard the rumors. You've just stated that dating doesn't interest you. So, tell us what your criteria for this baby daddy of yours?"

Sally looked away, took a long swallow of wine, and sighed. She knew getting out of this was going to prove far more difficult than just coming clean with the truth. "Okay, first, part of what you've heard may be true. Aimee knows my thoughts on this and has already tried to talk me out of it."

Liberty rolled her hand as if to say get on to the good stuff.

"Look, I've dated just about every guy in a sixty-mile radius of this town at one time or another."

All eyes were on her in the silent room.

"Long story, short."

"Yes, please," Liberty replied with a grin.

Sally held up her finger. "Healthy. Trustworthy."

"*That's* your second?" Liberty asked.

"I'm not looking for commitments. Truthfully, I had wanted to go with artificial insemination and do this alone. But the money I'd saved has been eaten up…by all of this." She gestured to the plastic strips covering her kitchen entrance. At the other end was a framework of her house where a wall was being torn down to create a family room at the back of the house. Sally shrugged and looked around at her friends. "I guess I figure there must be some guy out there who's not interested in the long term. Maybe someone I don't know very well, so it doesn't get awkward to run into him in town. I don't know, maybe even someone from out of town."

"That could be risky." Aimee frowned. "No, I don't like that idea at all."

Sally knew her friends meant well, but a team effort hadn't been in her plans, either. "This is something I need to work out on my own, okay? And I promise I won't do anything stupid."

The fresh log in the fireplace snapped, jarring everyone back from the unified silence.

"So, back to the auction?" Liberty said as she untangled from the blanket to skewer another marshmallow.

A thumping sound joined the whistling of the wind outdoors, causing them to look at each other. A knock, more urgent sounded at the front door.

Kaylee stifled a scream.

Curious as to who could possibly be out in the weather and at this hour, Sally grabbed a candle, and as an afterthought, her umbrella, by the door before she peeked through the peephole.

A large, dark silhouette stood on the porch. For a moment, she debated opening the door.

"Sally, open up. It's Clay Saunders."

Sally glanced over and saw her friends huddled together in the arched entrance to the front room.

"For God's sake, let the poor man in." Liberty pointed at the door, pulling Sally from her thoughts.

She unbolted the lock and the harsh wind snuffed out the candle even before she could open the door completely. Sally narrowed her eyes to the icy pelts of snow following Clay inside. He quickly hustled inside, his presence swallowing the space in the small foyer.

"Sorry it's so late. I had to stop and help this guy who'd gotten stuck in a snow drift."

He removed his knit hat and swept a gloved hand over his hair, sending icy crystals everywhere.

"What are you doing out in this?" Sally asked. "Come on in. Here, give me your coat. Come sit by the fire."

"I just came by for—that is, I think I might have left my tool belt in the kitchen."

"Your tool belt?" Sally asked, hanging up his coat as her friends paraded Clay to the chair closest to the fire.

Aimee dropped an afghan around his shoulders. Liberty offered him a glass of wine. He accepted the first, declined the second.

Sally stood in the foyer, unsure of what truck had just run over her.

"Uh…" Clay stood and shrugged off the blanket. "I remembered that I'd left it here. I might need it this weekend." He nodded, and then strode through the plastic curtain to the kitchen.

Liberty leaned over the couch and spoke in a whisper to Sally. "Go talk to him. Ask him to be in the auction."

Sally shook her head. Bad idea. With this guy's volatile temperament, she didn't feel it wise to put that kind of pressure on him.

"He's gorgeous," Kaylee whispered, staring where he stood beyond the translucent plastic. "Did you see that chest?"

"Looks aren't everything," Sally hissed in a low voice. She'd walked to the back of the couch, facing her friends with a determined stance. Deep down, she wondered if Clay had heard the rumors, or if he, too, bought into them. He didn't seem the type.

Aimee tilted her head and gave Sally the fish eye. "He is eligible and we need one more to complete the auction line-up."

"He certainly seems to have all the right equipment," Liberty said, raising a brow.

Sally stopped the idea with an upturned hand. "He wouldn't be interested, trust me." All eyes raised to look past her as she felt the wall of pure male body heat step up behind her. She looked up over her shoulder and smiled.

Clay hadn't realized Sally would be standing in the narrow path between the couch and the kitchen. The roomful of women staring at him, though, had him wondering what...or rather *who*, they'd been discussing. He was ex-Army. No fear. "Who wouldn't be interested, and in what?" he asked.

In the dim light it was difficult to register their expressions, but his gut cautioned that *he'd* been the topic of their conversation.

Sally turned quickly on her heel and caught him off-guard as she faced him. She folded her arms over her chest. "We were just saying how you'd probably not be interested in participating in the Spring Buckle Ball charity auction." Her words all but poked him in the chest with their absolute certainty.

Ah, yes, the infamous bachelor auction. It didn't appear that Sally was too thrilled about him being involved. Understandably, given their falling out last fall. Things had been left unresolved, which seemed to suit them both, since they'd barely spoken in the last few months. Time had served to ease some of the tension he'd first felt after arriving at the ranch. And while he had the sense that Sally was the type to forgive the things he'd blurted in his out of control frustration and anger, she quite likely hadn't forgotten.

He rubbed his hand over a days' worth of stubble on his cheek. Not exactly the best-looking example of a bachelor candidate, but maybe not the worst. He thought about what Tyler had mentioned regarding Sally and was curious whether it was true. Not that he was interested. God, no. If true, he thought it was the most cockamamie idea he'd ever heard, not to mention irresponsible and dangerous.

He cleared his throat, glanced around the room at the indistinguishable faces, then looked down at Sally. Her chin raised in stubborn defiance barely cleared his shoulder, but positioned her tempting mouth at an excellent angle.

He blinked. He might be her saving grace. The only guy in town who wasn't trying to audition for her crazy plan. If this gossip kept on the path it was headed, it was clear that every guy in a three-county radius could making life pretty difficult for her. At least, it's what he told himself before he opened his mouth. "Sure." He shrugged. "What do I have to do?"

"Yee haw," Liberty pumped her fist in the air.

Clay heard a muffled giggle from the girl Tyler had been eyeing at Dusty's bar. He brought his gaze back to Sally's, whose mouth resembled a bass. She stared at him. Maybe he'd spoken too soon, because another thought, far more disturbing, occurred to him. "Okay, wait a second. This isn't one of those *Magic Mike* kind of auctions, right?"

Liberty clapped her hands and uttered a feminine squeal. "What a fabulous idea! That would really pack them in. You should consider that option, Sally."

"Liberty?" Sally said. "Seriously?" She tossed her friend a stern look.

"What? You've got to admit. It would certainly liven up things."

"No," Sally repeated as though disciplining a student. She looked at Clay. "No, it's nothing like that. The annual Montana Buckle Ball is the Business Chamber's Spring gala, dinner and dance. Apparently a few years back they decided to go from a silent raffle auction to the bachelor auction where we feature some of the area's finest single men."

He held in a smile, wanting to tell her he appreciated the compliment, but he was pretty damn sure she was being muscled-armed into this decision.

"The proceeds from the auction each year goes to a worthy cause in the area," Angelique interjected. "This year the Women and Children's shelter in Billings has been chosen as recipient."

"The chamber takes the applicants we've suggested, but they must first meet certain criteria before they're officially accepted." Sally kept her gaze on his. "Those chosen must agree to be the winning bidder's date for the remainder of the evening."

That was it? If he didn't know better, it sounded as though Sally was making it sound as difficult as possible to go through with this. Which, of course, pissed him off enough to shove that challenge right back at Little Miss Bossy Butt. "I'm in, then. Thank you, ladies." He purposely avoided eye contact with Sally. He knew his presence in the event had thrown a wrench into her plans, but what the hell. He grinned. He still had to pass muster with the chamber. He looked back, resting his gaze on Sally. "That is, of course, if the chamber approves me."

The lights flickered again and suddenly he found himself staring into Sally's beautiful eyes. Her cheeks, he noted, were noticeably flushed. "I should probably go."

"I'll show you to the door," she offered in a curt tone.

"Ladies." Clay nodded and followed Sally to the foyer. She stood ready, her hand on the doorknob. He couldn't get his coat zipped up and his gloves on fast enough.

She opened the door and a rush of icy snow blew in as though blown through the screen by a wind machine. A yelp sounded from the other room even as the pictures hung along the stairwell clattered and fell to the floor.

Aimee appeared in the entry. "Close that door! Look the snow is blowing in."

Sally struggled against the rugged wind and the small drift of snow that edged against the bottom of the door and along the hall toward the back of the house. Snow swirled around her stocking feet. Clay reached out and grabbed the door, shoving it shut with his shoulder. He released a sigh as he leaned against it.

"Well, you certainly can't go out in that." Aimee fisted her hands on her hips.

Clay wasn't terribly excited about the prospect either, but one look at Sally's face gave him pause about the alternatives.

Liberty appeared at Aimee's side. "What kind of person would turn someone out on a night like this?" Clay caught Liberty's not-so-subtle nudge.

He brushed the snow from where it clung to his eyelashes. "Tyler's place is just a few blocks from here."

Liberty spoke first. "That's ridiculous. You're already here, where its safe and warm."

The lights flickered once again, then they were plunged into darkness.

"Seems like we have our answer, then," Aimee stated. "Sally, he can use the couch, right? Since we're all bunking upstairs?"

"Well, yes. I suppose…."

Clay held up his hand. "Okay, ladies, I have to confess something. Rein asked me to stop by and check in on you. I honestly think, that given the circumstances, he would prefer if I were to stay. Just in case."

Small flickers of light began to appear in the sitting room. Kaylee appeared with a candle. "I don't know about you all, but if there's a vote, then I say he stays."

Clay looked at the floor and chanced a look at Sally. "Only if Sally is comfortable with the idea." He waited, closely watching her expression.

"I'll get you a pillow and blanket." She reached for the candle Kaylee held and started up the stairs.

"Sally?"

She paused, looking over her shoulder at him. She was a damn fine-looking woman in bright daylight, but in candlelight she could stop a man's heart. "Thank you. I'll go get some more firewood."

She nodded and, without discussion, went upstairs.

As it turned out, Rein and his brothers were indeed relieved to hear he'd stayed. Not that he was much help, other than to bring in firewood. He sat on a kitchen chair and listened to more about this Buckle Ball.

Sally's organizational skills mystified him. She seemed to have the details of this event down to a gnat's eyebrow and given the willing ladies around her, she wasn't afraid to delegate, showing the skills of a firm leader. They hadn't asked much for his thoughts over the next couple of hours, but he was content to drink some orange juice and watch the five friends. Their laughter, inside jokes, and animated conversation reminded him of his squad, and better times.

Sometime later, the group, now tired, began to drift up the stairs. Sally was the last to go up after checking both the front and back doors. The electricity hadn't come back on yet, and while the house was chilly, it was tolerable with a layering of clothes.

"Are you going to be okay on the couch?" she asked as she watched him unfold the blankets she'd brought down.

He glanced at her and tipped his head toward the blazing fire. "I feel kind of bad that I've got this. You sure you ladies are going to be all right up there?"

"Hey, five women snuggled together in a king bed. We'll be like bugs in a rug."

Clay raised his brows. "Can't argue with that." He snapped open another blanket. "Hopefully, the utility company will have the power back up by sunrise."

She nodded. "Okay, then. Goodnight."

Clay bit his lip in thought, glancing at her departing form. Hell, he had no idea if this was a good time or not, but he spoke before he could consider otherwise. "Sally? Have you got a minute? I wanted to speak with you."

She placed her hand on the rail and looked at the steps before she turned to look at him. "It's been a really long week and I'm beat. Maybe it could wait until another time?"

Clay shrugged, averting his gaze to hide his disappointment. "Absolutely. It's not important. You get some rest and thanks again for letting me crash here."

He turned his back and tugged his shirt from his jeans as he sat down, shrugging out of his flannel shirt and down to his faded T-shirt with *Army* across his chest. He considered the wisdom of removing his leg and, laying back on the couch, decided to leave it on. He cradled his hand under his head and propped his good leg over the arm of the couch. Which he realized in short order was a vintage Victorian-type sitting room couch, just barely wider than his torso. He shifted, pulled the blanket over his shoulders and closed his eyes. Dreams—nightmares—mostly, were hit and miss these days, depending on his mood and how much he had to drink before retiring

"You know, we can move the cushions to the floor and add more blankets to make a more comfortable pallet for you."

He opened his eyes and met Sally's gaze peering down at him from over the camelback couch. "I'm good, really. Just grateful that you chose not to kick me out in this." He offered her a friendly smile.

She walked around the end of the couch and knelt to stir the waning fire, bringing it back to a roaring blaze and radiating heat in the small room.

He sat up as Sally nestled in her overstuffed reading chair and pulled an afghan around her.

"I want to make this a piano room. Give lessons," she said as she stared into the fire.

Curious, he nudged more conversation from her. "I thought you were sleepy?" It seemed clear to him that she wasn't entirely comfortable with him being in her house, or she had a lot on her mind.

"I am." She stifled a yawn. "But I can't sleep."

Clay chuckled. "I'd offer to trade you spots, but I'm pretty sure that wouldn't go over well." He cleared his throat and smiled when he heard her quiet laugh. She sat with her chin propped on her hand, staring into the fire.

"Hey, as long as you're here, I wanted to clear the air and apologize for some of the things I said that first day on the ranch." Clay took a deep breath and waited, leaving it open-ended in hopes that she would respond in kind.

She didn't.

He pushed on, feeling it was better to clear the air between them, especially if he became involved with the auction. "That day...well, I was going through a really bad time." He hated the way it sounded as though he was making excuses for his behavior. Life here had helped him—through self-study, some visits with a doc in Billings, and the work and people at the ranch, he was better able now to understand the triggers to some of his anger issues. His survivor's guilt still taunted him from time to time, but some of the nightmares had subsided to where he could go one or two nights without a sleep aid.

"I understand," she replied, glancing at him. "You don't need to explain."

That particular response was, in fact, one of his triggers. He swiped his hand over his mouth. That was the thing. Folks back here, most don't *really* understand having to look at what was left of your team, your buddies—in pieces—strewn over the sand. Clay swallowed and rubbed his hand over the top of his thigh. He'd forgotten to take some meds to ease the muscle strain of his new leg. "You don't really understand, Sally. I'm sorry, but not many do, not unless you've been there."

She looked at him then, with a steady gaze that he couldn't read.

"You know I can't even remember very well what triggered that exchange," she said, her brows furrowed in thought as she peered at him.

"You probably didn't say or do anything out of the ordinary, Sally."

She laughed softly. "Yeah, my dad used to say I could be as prickly as a cactus some days."

Clay studied her. "Don't be so hard on yourself. We all have our moments. God knows I've had my share."

She shrugged. "I suppose you're right." She sighed, stood, and dropped her afghan on the chair. She walked over and sat on the edge of the couch, careful, he noted, not to sit too close. "So, let's just say, that we were both having a bad day and neither one of us meant anything we said."

Clay grinned. "You really didn't mean it when you called me a spoiled brat and I needed to cowboy up?"

She grinned sheepishly "Damn, I'd hoped you'd forgotten."

"I have a good memory. It's a blessing and a curse," Clay said. At least they'd made some headway into chipping away at the frozen wall between them. "Honestly, I arrived here carrying a whole lot of self-pity. Everybody was just being friendly, trying to make me feel welcome that first day, and I shut it all out. I didn't want to feel good. I mistook everyone's kindness for pity, like I was a charity case."

She nodded. "That helps to explain calling me Little Miss Bossy Butt in front of everyone and telling me to mind my own damn business." She looked up in thought. "And something about not needing anything from some backwoods grade school music teacher—or something along those lines."

Clay's face crumpled into a grimace. "Your memory is pretty good." He looked down and sighed. "Honestly, you were probably right at the time, calling me out like that." He looked at her. "I am better—emotionally stronger. Being here at the ranch has helped tremendously. Just feeling productive—moving forward with my life." He released a sigh. "I think I was in a lot of denial still. Mad at the world in general. If it's any consolation, Rein, Dalton, and poor Hank, got the brunt of that part of me back then as well. I'm damn lucky for their patience and friendship, that they reminded me of the man they knew as their friend in college."

Her gaze searched his before she spoke. "Life changes for sure. Sometimes, it's hard to remember in those moments the things inside us that make us truly good."

Clay thought on her words, and then held out his hand with a smile. "Truce?"

She accepted his hand and, to his delight, smiled. "Truce, at least until the next time I need to kick your butt."

He chuckled. "Fair enough, bossy butt." This conversation, much to his relief, had taken a great weight from his shoulders. That said—he wasn't sure she was prepared yet to hear his thoughts on the recent "baby daddy" rumors circling around town. What he did notice was that she hadn't yet released his hand. She was smiling at him.

"What?" Not that he minded one bit holding her hand or having her beautiful smile directed at him.

"It's just that I haven't felt this good about being friends with a guy in a long time. I hadn't realized how much I missed it."

Being her perceived big brother was all well and good in theory, but the tightening below his belt proved otherwise.

"Sally," he said, brushing his thumb over the back of her hand. "I heard something today that I wanted to ask you about." He waded into the 'baby daddy' waters, not wanting to disrupt what progress they'd made.

Her eyes widened and she tugged her hand from his, bolting toward the stairs. "We really need to get some rest."

"Sally?" He shifted to look at her as she walked hurriedly away.

She paused on the stairs, tapped the railing gently, and then looked at him. "Please don't ruin it." She held his gaze. "Goodnight, Clay."

CHAPTER FOUR

Sally pushed back the hair from her face. She'd waded to the back of the walk-in closet, climbing over boxes and plastic tubs that she kept telling herself she'd have to go through one of these days. Today wasn't that day. But her suitcases, at least a decade old, were stuffed at the very back of the closet. Which reminded her how often she'd gotten out of this little town.

"Hey, are you in here?" Rein stuck his head inside the door. The bare bulb with its yellowed string pull illuminated the spot just inside the door, and little else. She looked over her shoulder and saw him searching for her in the shadows. "Sal, you need a flashlight?"

"I'm good," she answered. She knew exactly where the suitcases were stored. Her knee bumped against the sharp corner of an ornate frame. "Ow, dammit," she muttered. She'd forgotten about the old mirror that her mother had once hung above the fireplace mantel.

"Do you need any help?"

She planted her hands on the stack of containers stacked between her and her set of tweed Samsonite luggage. It had been a graduation gift from high school—for college and beyond. Wide-eyed and full of adventure, she couldn't wait to taste college life, to be on her own—away from the arguments between her parents that had then plagued her daily life. She had dreams of visiting places where music was born—Europe, New York, New Orleans. As it turned out, she returned instead to End of the Line to take care of her dad. The suitcases hadn't been anywhere since.

She prayed that her fingers wouldn't come into contact with any cobwebs. The saving grace was that most eight-legged critters were either dead or snuggled in for the winter.

She groped for the handle, draping her body over the massive containers. After her father died, she'd taken down the majority of his possessions and nearly all the decorative items he'd kept around the house, even after her mother left and stuffed them into all these storage tubs. Closing each one and hauling them to the far end of the closet, she told herself she'd need to go through it and keep the things she really wanted and send the rest to the Goodwill bin that Nan over at the sporting goods store had set up recently in the corner of her parking lot. She growled as she searched for the handle, stretching her reach as far as she could.

"Got it!" she called out with glee, unsure if Rein was still around or not. It didn't matter. Tiny victories. Now if it still held together, life would be good. She yanked the massive suitcase from its spot wedged between tubs and the wall. Stumbling backwards over more storage boxes, she lay for a moment, suitcase atop her, staring at the ceiling, seeing the shadowy beginnings of cracks from the house settling. Was she smart to be investing so much into renovating the old house?

"I heard a thud, Sally. You okay back there?" Rein's voice came from the door, the view impeded by the racks of clothing hung on both sides of the narrow closet.

She struggled with the suitcase and, after hauling it over a few more obstacles, smiled as she found her way back to the door.

Rein backed away and let her through. "You know they're still looking for Jimmy Hoffa." He eyed her suitcase, as large as an old steamer trunk.

"What? It's still in good shape…I think." She grabbed the handle and it fell off in her hand. "I probably yanked on it too hard."

He studied the luggage, not bothering to mask his skepticism.

"There's another handle on the side." Sally said. "It'll be fine."

"You're not crossing the Atlantic, Sal. It's a week, maybe a week and a half, tops, and it's not as though you can't stop by and pick up whatever you need every day." He rubbed the back of his neck and glanced at her.

"Ok, I realize it appears that I may be going away for longer, but this is all I've got other than garbage bags."

Rein shrugged.

"Which I refuse to pack my clothes in, thank you." Sally swiped off a thin layer of dust over the top of the case. "Besides, with the weird weather we've been having, I don't know what kind of clothing I'll need—or what kind of shoes, for that matter.

He let out a sigh, the kind that meant surrender. "Fine by me. Get her loaded and for God's sake, don't try to lift that thing. Call down and one of us will get it to the truck for you. Is it me, or is it listing?" He tipped his head and nudged it. "Looks like you're missing one of the wheels."

"Thanks." She eyed him as he left, then hauled the monstrosity to the bed. Careful of what might leap out, she opened it, scanned the inside, and decided to lay out a clean sheet as a barrier between it and her clothing. She made a mental note to purchase a new set of luggage—if there was any money left after the renovations. Her stash that she'd held onto for years—the small inheritance her dad had left her—had been slowly dwindling with the hidden costs of renovations.

Aimee appeared at the bedroom door. "Hey, I had an appointment in town today with Doc Johnson. Thought I'd stop by and see if you needed any help packing." Aimee walked in and sat down beside the suitcase. "I won't lie, I'm kind of excited to have you visiting for a few days." She looked at the case, then at Sally. "It *is* a few days, right?"

Sally tossed her a side look and noticed she looked a little pale. She grabbed an armful of undergarments from the top drawer, and dumped them in the suitcase. "Doc Johnson? Everything okay?

Aimee stood and walked over to Sally's reading chair. "Did you want to take these?" She scooped up two cardigans draped over the back.

"Yes, go ahead and put them in," Sally answered, heading to her closet. She picked out a number of interchangeable pieces and turned to find Aimee meticulously folding the cardigans. She hadn't responded yet about her doctor visit. "Aimee?"

Her friend looked up as though she'd been lost in her thoughts. "Hum? I'm sorry. I was thinking about something else, did you say something?"

Sally noticed then the dark circles under her friend's eyes. She scooted the suitcase and sat on the end of the bed. She patted the spot beside her. "Sit."

Aimee sighed, but did as Sally requested. She held one of Sally's sweaters, plucking at a loose string.

"Aimee, you're not sick are you? You'd tell me if it was something like that, right?" An old familiar hollow feeling swallowed Sally's insides, like the time her mother had fist told her about her dad's diagnosis of multiple sclerosis.

Aimee touched her shoulder. "Oh, honey. No, no I'm fine… I will be, anyway, as soon as I get over the shock."

Sally narrowed her gaze. "Jesus, Mary, and Joseph. You're pregnant."

Aimee's eyes welled. She nodded.

Relief flooded Sally and she let out the breath she'd not realized she was holding in. "What great news! I'm so happy for you. And *omigod*, my little Gracie is going to be a big sister." She wrapped her arms around her friend. It had been more than a couple of weeks since their girl's night out.

"I wasn't sure how to tell you." Aimee sniffed with her face muffled against Sally's shoulder.

Sally held her at arm's length, searching her face. "Oh, sweetheart, I couldn't be happier. I'm over the moon. Does Wyatt know yet?" she asked.

"Not yet. I'll tell him tonight. But he'll want to tell everyone at dinner on Sunday."

"Of course. This is wonderful news." Sally hugged her friend again. "But no more margaritas for you for a while. How far along are you?"

"Not very. I'd taken a home test the other day after the smell of bacon made me queasy. I thought I'd gag. And you know how the Kinnison men love their bacon. Wyatt will cook up two pounds if he thinks Michael is stopping by for breakfast."

Having waitressed in high school at Betty's, Sally had seen her share of meat lover breakfast platters going out to most of the male population in End of the Line. Where cattle ranching reigned supreme and hunting was the number one sport, there was little doubt as to why.

"Please don't mention this yet." Aimee looked at Sally. "Especially not to Rein or Betty, for goodness sake. It'll get to Wyatt before I can." Aimee brushed the shine of tears from her cheeks. "Enough about me. What'd you find out with your visit to the fertility clinic?" Aimee shifted to face her, checking over her shoulder to be sure no one was in earshot.

Unfortunately, the news was not nearly as wonderful as her friend's. "Well, I've discovered there are a lot of people who are apparently having difficulty having children. So count your blessings."

Aimee smoothed her hand over her still flat stomach. "I do…every day."

Sally had brought home a handful of brochures on protocol, insurance, and break-down of costs with each stage of the IVF process. She dug them out of her book bag and handed them to Aimee. "I haven't had a chance to look at those in great detail, but bottom line, it appears that it's going to cost in the neighborhood of between eleven to fifteen thousand for in-vitro fertilization—and that's if everything goes according to plan the first time."

"Yes, but you're healthy." Aimee studied one of the pamphlets. "You've had your check-up this year, your periods are normal—everything seems to be in working order, right?"

Sally nodded. "It's not really my health that concerns me. There are so many other expenses I hadn't really considered. Costs of the donor sperm, agency fees, legal fees—and then there are the injections I have to give myself." She eyed Aimee with a grimace. "And you know how terrified I am of needles."

"What does that do?" Aimee asked.

"It's supposed to increase the number of eggs. Not every egg is optimum, I guess. And they can freeze the good ones—part of the costs—if things don't go well the first time."

Her friend looked at her, shock registering on her face. "You mean this is the cost for one time?"

"Not entirely, but it's a financial commitment," Sally answered with a shrug. "And there is no doubt each of these kids is truly, desperately wanted."

Aimee nodded. "Wow." She shuffled through the brochures, then glanced at Sally. "I don't mean to be nosy, but can you afford this? I mean, I know you really want a child of your own."

"I checked and my health insurance covers most of the preliminary costs—tests, office visits, evaluation." She released a quiet sigh. "Then the real fun begins." Sally gave her friend a weak smile, trying not to let her disappoint show. She should be content. She was healthy. There was still the chance she could meet someone and have kids of her own. Women these days were having kids in their forties. The number of scenarios had played over and over in her mind and the answer, it seemed, always fell to the bottom line. One that was slowly being eaten away by the renovations to update this old house and make it a safe and efficient place to raise a child. "It's certainly given me a lot to think about." Sally stood and resumed her packing. "I'm sorry. Come on, put those down and let's not let this put a damper on your good news, okay? Besides, I'd like to get to my cabin before nightfall so I can get settled."

Aimee nodded. "Sounds like a plan. Where to next?"

Sally pointed to the dresser. "Everything in the second and third drawers... oh, and grab that robe off the back of the door, please. I'm going to start in the bathroom."

"Did Rein seem to think this phase would take long?" Aimee called out to her.

"A week, he thought. Guess it depends on what they find. This old house has already coughed up a few surprises. Tyler is still waiting on my sink. He must have ordered it from another continent." Sally dropped her hair dryer and cosmetic bag in the suitcase.

"I can't believe this is almost full," Aimee remarked as they stood shoulder to shoulder staring at the suitcase.

Sally folded the extra sheeting over her clothes as though wrapping a gift. "There." She smiled, tugged the lid down, and zipped it shut.

Aimee grabbed it, preparing to haul it off the bed. Sally stopped her.

"Get away from that, you crazy woman," she scolded. "You grab my pillows and book bag."

Aimee shoved the bag over her shoulder and grabbed the pillows.

Granted, the full suitcase was much heavier than she'd thought it would be. Akin to a load of bricks came to mind as Sally braced one knee on the bed and pulled the suitcase to the edge, prepared to let it simply fall to the floor.

A large hand clamped down over hers on the handle. "Step aside, I'll get that."

She felt the heat of Clay's all-male body behind her. Frustrated that her life wasn't exactly going as planned, her ire rose. By golly, she'd been on her own for years, taken care of her dad, and scores of every type of kid—she ought to be able to handle a damn suitcase. "You know, I'm not a helpless damsel in distress."

"Never said you were," Clay replied calmly.

"Just so we're clear, I have been known to move a baby grand by myself." She glanced over her shoulder, eyeing him.

He leveled her a look. "On wheels, congratulations," he said. "And news flash, this isn't a competition."

"I'll just take this stuff on downstairs," Aimee piped up. "I want to talk to Rein about Sunday night."

Sally peeked around Clay and waved. He hadn't budged an inch. She was still trapped on the bed between him and the suitcase. "Thanks, Aimee." She looked up and met his steady gaze. He gave her a thin-lipped smile before he spoke. "You going to let me get this, bossy butt?" He grinned then. Mr. funny guy.

"Be careful. The other handle broke. I can't really vouch for this one." She scooted backwards, avoiding eye contact as she slithered off the bed and inched around him. Grabbing her house slippers and pressing them against her chest to hide how he'd affected her, she watched him lift the suitcase, seemingly with little effort, and stand it upright, where it listed precariously. Luckily, he caught it before it fell.

Clearly a matter of leverage. She turned to walk ahead of him down the stairs.

"Need these?"

She turned and her heart stilled. He stood at the top of the steps, holding the stack of brochures out to her.

"They were lying on the bed. Figured you might need them."

She snatched them quickly from him. "Thanks, I've been doing a little research for a friend of mine." She averted her eyes from his, hoping he'd bought what she was trying to sell.

Yeah, he hadn't bought that line about researching for a friend. Sally had been avoiding him since she arrived at the ranch. She'd begged off the traditional family dinner the night after she arrived, stating she had work to do for school and needed to get herself settled.

She was bunked in the first cabin nearest to the main house on the asphalt roadway, while he was in the last cabin, farthest from everything. He'd wanted the privacy and just outside his door was the creek than ran through the back of the Kinnison property and the dense forest that covered the foothills. When weather permitted, he enjoyed sitting on his patio out back, taking in the stars, letting the quiet seep into his pores when his memories became too much to ignore. Rein had given him full use of the mini utility farm cart for tooling around the ranch, but he enjoyed the walk when the path was clear.

He'd been busy the past week, up at dawn to help with chores, and then off to Sally's house with Rein to work on her renovations. Those brochures and the rumor Tyler had spoken to him about filtered in and out of his brain. The Montana Spring Buckle Ball was two weeks away and he and Rein were busting their butts to get Sally moved back home before then.

"Hey, guys," Tyler called from Sally's back door. "The sink's here."

Clay looked over his shoulder and saw Tyler with a two-wheel dolly standing at the open end of Sally's new kitchen. The water line had been re-routed, electrical lines updated and replaced. Sally's new island with a yawning gap in the center sat gleaming, awaiting the finishing touch.

"Fantastic," Rein said, dropping the drill he'd been using on the new hood range. "Gentlemen, I think we're going to be out of here by Monday at the latest." He looked around. "Just about a week." He grinned.

Tyler unstrapped the box and stood looking at what had been accomplished. "Sally's going to love this. Taking out this back wall really has made a difference. And turning her dad's old bedroom back here into a family room is a great idea. Now she can cook and keep an eye on her kid." He glanced their way. "Whenever that should happen." Tyler viewed the room with his hands over his chest, unaware that Rein was staring at him.

Clay raised his eyebrows. This was going to get interesting.

"What are you talking about?" Rein asked. "Sally doesn't have any kids, you know that." He picked up the drill and resumed his task.

"Oh, come on, everyone's talking about it." Tyler fished out his box cutter and began to open the box.

Clay kept his eyes on the cabinet hinges, wanting to caution Tyler to shut his pie-hole. The guy seemed to have few, if any, filters.

Rein's drill stopped.

Both Clay and Tyler looked up. Clay scratched his chin—by the look on Rein's face, this was not going to bode well for Tyler.

"Geez. Why are you looking at me?" he said. "I didn't start it. I only heard about it."

"Didn't start what? Just heard—*what*, exactly?" Rein turned to face Tyler.

"You know, that Sally's looking for a guy to father her child."

Holy mother of God. Clay reached over and gently took the drill from Rein's hand. There was a moment when it seemed the air in the house was sucked into a vacuum, and then Rein was in front of Tyler, grabbing him by his shirt. He pushed his face into the shocked plumber's face. "I hope to hell you're stopping any kind of shit like that you're hearing, Tyler."

Clay straightened, prepared to intervene if things got ugly.

Tyler turned a pale shade of chalk. "Really? You hadn't heard?" He chuckled lightly. "I guess not."

Clay could all but see Rein reeling in his fury.

Rein took a deep breath and stepped back, though his fist still held a wad of Tyler's shirt. "I think you best go. And if I hear that you're helping spread this crap, you'll have me to answer to. Are we clear?" He dropped his hold.

Confusion clouded Tyler's expression. "I don't know what you're so upset about. I didn't start it. I overheard it at Betty's the other day" He glanced at Clay. "Isn't that what I told you the other night at Dusty's?"

Rein stopped rubbing his temple and looked at Clay. "Jesus, you've heard this, too?"

Clay decided to keep the information about the brochures close to the hip. "Just what Tyler mentioned. But I don't get around town much."

"I've got to talk with Sally and apologize," Rein said, looking out the kitchen window. "Wyatt and I were sitting at Betty's the other day and he was mentioning something about Sally wanting a child of her own." He shook his head. "Clearly, someone overheard and has decided to fill in the blanks with their own version."

Tyler brushed down the front of his shirt. "I thought it was common knowledge. Hell, I'd offer my services to Sal in a heartbeat, if I thought she'd give me the time of day."

Rein's gaze snapped to Tyler's.

"Purely out of friendship." He put up his hands in defense. "For Sally, I'd do anything."

"The out of friendship, maybe you should start focusing on setting people straight if you hear this rumor again." Clay suggested quietly. "That kind of talk could affect her job. Besides, it's nobody's business what Sally chooses to do with her life."

Rein and Tyler stared at him. "You agree she should raise a kid by herself?" Rein asked.

At what point the tide had turned, Clay wasn't sure. "Hell, no. I think it's insane. It's hard enough to raise a kid with both parents."

Rein nodded. "You're right about her job. Principle Kale can be a hard-ass. And rumors in this town seem to take on a life of their own once they get fuel under them."

Clay shrugged. "It happens. People mean well. They're curious about one of their own. Everyone wants to think they're helping, but it can get out of control and pretty soon everyone has their own spin on it."

"I'm sorry, Rein. I don't want Sally getting hurt."

Rein nodded. "I know, Tyler. Sorry, man. I'm as mad at myself really. I should know better not to discuss sensitive stuff over at Betty's. You never know who may overhear your conversation." He released a sigh. "Come on, let's get this done so she can have at least this much that's back to normal in her life." Rein looked from Tyler to Clay. "I'll talk to Sally, but you guys help squash anything you hear, okay? I'll let Betty know, too. That way she can stop what she may hear, and I know she will."

Clay was curious as to whether or not Rein had spoken to Sally. He'd seen her a couple of times from the barn as she headed off to school. Each time she'd been wearing that mass of gorgeous red hair secured with a clip that seemed more like a prison sentence for her locks, in his opinion.

The weather had turned unseasonably mild for Montana in February. Having lived in Texas and California longer than he had Montana, his body wasn't as used to the cold as the locals here in the mountain town. Michael Greyfeather blamed it on global warming, Clay was just grateful that the bitter north winds had subsided and his muscles didn't seem to ache as badly. That, however, was nothing compared to the blazing fury of a woman late for her trail ride. Wyatt and the four kids from the Women and Children's shelter in Billings had saddled up and were waiting as Sally's beat-up truck came sailing down the long drive, kicking up bits of ice and gravel as she came to a halt in front of her cabin.

Clay eyed her as she flew into her cabin, and a short time later emerged in her riding clothes, tugging a jacket over her arms. She grabbed the reins to the horse he'd been saddling for her and, before he could get a word out, she dropped her boot in the stirrup. "Sally, wait, I'm…."

Yeah, it wasn't pretty. He scratched his jaw. She was loaded for bear, that much was true. The saddle listed and she wound up on her butt on the frozen mud, foot still stuck in the stirrup.

She looked up at him with a dazed look that dissolved into fury. Clay bit back a laugh. Damn, little bossy butt.

"Didn't Michael teach you how to properly saddle a horse?"

He casually reached over and unhooked her boot from the stirrup and righted the loose saddle. "Pardon me, but you didn't really give me a chance to tell you I wasn't finished yet." He offered her a hand. She slapped her gloved palm to his begrudgingly and he hauled her to her feet.

She glanced at him, those green-gold eyes meeting his as she wiped the dirt off her backside. He'd thought to offer his help, but changed his mind. Clay glanced at his feet, concealing a smile as he maneuvered the blankets and saddle over the horse's back.

"Feel free not to choke on that laugh, Mr. Saunders." She nudged him aside and started tightening the cinches. The horse snorted and stamped his hoof, seemingly taking sides in Sally's displeasure.

He cleared his throat, then stepped forward and nudged her out of the way. "You can just simmer down—" The nickname he'd given her teetered on the edge of his tongue.

Her gaze held his in challenge.

"Why don't you give me five minutes to finish." He glanced over his shoulder. "You seem a little preoccupied." Clay didn't claim to be psychic, but he sure as hell felt her ire.

"You know, despite what everyone seems to think around here, I can manage quite well on my own."

No doubt, Clay thought, but didn't back down, reminding himself that Miss Bossy Butt was in some kind of mood today and curious if it was only that she was running late. Still, he breathed a quiet sigh when she stepped aside and leaned against the nearby fence. She brushed errant strands of hair from her face, looking off into the distance. Worry was etched on her beautiful face. "Everything coming together for the ball?" he asked casually. Tightening the harness, he smoothed the blanket under the saddle for the horse's comfort.

"Hum? I'm sorry, uh, yes, things seem to be coming together." She hadn't looked at him, instead raising a hand to Wyatt as though to say she'd be right there. It was usually Michael who went along on the trail rides because of his familiarity of the area, and he loved to entertain the kids with stories of folk and animal lore.

"That's good." Small talk. Clay had difficulty enough with long discussions unless it happened to involve a deck of cards and a cold beer. Small talk? Not his thing.

"By the way, you have your tux, right?" she asked in an urgent tone.

He finished adjusting the stirrup, wanting to remind her that he'd heard of his acceptance—not from her—but from Maggie, the owner of the newspaper and a member of chamber committee. It'd been clear to him from the night of the blizzard that she wasn't fully convinced of his inclusion. Now she cared to check up on him? "Ms. Andersen," Clay said. "In case you hadn't noticed, I'm a big boy. And whatever the hell has your panties in a twist, you can just tone it down. You need someone to listen to whatever the hell is eating you—fine. I'll be happy to. But cut with the attitude. Lady. It doesn't look good on you."

She looked at him as though he'd slapped her.

"There you go. She's ready." He eyed her shocked expression. "Need a lift up?"

Without a word, she took the reins and he stepped back to offer her plenty of room. She grabbed the saddle horn and paused. "I could use the lift, please. If it's not too much trouble."

He bent down, offered his clasped hands, and lifted her to mount the horse.

She toyed with the reins, then glanced at him, her demeanor far more contrite. "I'm sorry I seem a little edgy today, Mr. Saunders."

He tossed her a smile. "I'm sorry you got your backside dirty when you fell."

She nodded.

Dammit. The woman was a quandary for certain—bossy, unstoppable one minute and soft and vulnerable, the next. He reached out, taking the reins and stopped her quiet departure. "So you can relax. Yes, I have my tux…on a hanger, by the way, ready to go."

She searched his eyes, then sighed. "I have so much on my mind. You just happened to be here and got the brunt of it. I'm sorry."

Clay shrugged. "Apology accepted on one condition."

She raised her brow and looked down at him. He had to blink to jump-start his brain. He had to stop this—it wasn't helping him sleep any better at night. "I think it's time we call each other by our first names." He held out his hand. "Hello, my name is Clay." To his amazement, she accepted it.

"Sally."

He nodded, dropped his hand and his hold on the horse. "See, that was fairly painless, wasn't it?"

She didn't answer. Instead, she jerked the reins and trotted across to where the group waited for her.

Head down, Clay walked back to the barn. The woman, though pretty as a summer sunset, had the personality of a damn cactus. Beautiful to look at— dangerous if you got too close. Not that the idea had crossed his mind… more than twice that day.

Women, as a rule, still baffled him. The come-to-Jesus realization hit him after being released from the hospital and going back to stay for a time with his sister, her accountant husband, and their two boys. Sunny California. Warm sunshine. Beautiful beaches. A slice of home. If there'd been a worse mistake than surviving the damn rocket grenade, it was seeing the look of pity on his sister's face, the day the cab dumped him on her doorstep.

"Clay!" Julie squealed. Her enthusiasm waned as her gaze traveled the length of him and lingered on his new leg. Granted, sticking out from the khaki cargo shorts it did seem to have a little 'terminator" vibe. It was California. Everyone wears shorts, right?

He smiled, though it didn't seem to lessen the tightness in his chest.

His sister, blinked as though jarred from her thoughts. "Let me help you with that." She reached for the duffle bag slung over his shoulder.

Her husband, still in a white shirt and tie, appeared beside Julie. "Jesus, Clay, I'm so sorry I couldn't get to the airport in time to pick you up. Here, let me help you with that." He nudged his wife. "That's far too heavy for you, babe."

Clay glanced over the pair quietly chiding each other and saw his nephews frozen in place at the bottom of the stairs inside. He jerked the bag from their grasp and dropped it at his feet. "I'm not helpless. I can carry my own damn bag." The words exploded from him before he realized it. They said that might happen if he encountered the right triggers. Being pitied—he'd soon discover—was one of those triggers. Realizing he stood on their front steps still he glanced over and caught the shocked gaze of a neighbor. They cast a strange look his way. Clay snorted. He hadn't slept well since his return, he was adjusting to a new mechanical leg, and he hadn't shaved for a few days. All-in-all, he felt like a homeless man, seeking a handout.

It took only until the second week at his sisters to realize how uncomfortable she was around him. The discomfort trickled down to his nephew's every time their questions were silenced. He tried to give his sister some slack. She was carrying a lot on her plate while he'd been deployed—a home, husband gone all the time, two kids, and their mom, who was now in an Alzheimer's care facility nearby. That *alone had to have been difficult, it was for Clay the first few times he'd gone to visit her.*

"I have a son. His name is Clay, also. He's in the war, you know. Army-man, like his grandfather." She'd smile sweetly at him, then her gaze would drift out the window to the birdhouse beyond. Clay would sit and stare at her, so small and fragile, not the fierce Texas-born woman he'd once known-who could strike the fear of God in him with one look. It damn near killed him and he couldn't go back. The fact that she didn't recognize him drove deep into his psyche, already littered with enough garbage to clean up. He leapt at Hanks suggestion about coming to Montana, to some ranch that a couple of their college friends owned. What other choice did he have? At least until he'd gotten some things straightened out inside him. Then maybe he'd head back to his home state of Texas and settle down.

"Sally has a strong spirit."

Clay was jarred from his memories by Michael's comment as he walked into the barn that had been built to stable the overflow of rescued horses from the Mountain Sunrise ranch over the winter months. Tying into the purpose of the Kinnison legacy of the Last Hope Ranch, Michael Greyfeather—once the head ranch hand and good friend to Jed Kinnison— had suggested to Jed's sons that they partner with the equine rescue ranch, where Michael had once worked. To help in housing the horses that had been rehabilitated and were now awaiting *forever* families—the ranch would continue to check with the families and if caring for the horse didn't work out, they would take them back at the ranch. The concept, readily accepted by the Kinnsion brothers, had already served to help in many areas, not only in Last Hope Ranch guests assisting in the care and nurturing of the horses, but also enabling special trail rides for kids who might never have the chance to be around a horse. It was a win-win situation, but the need for housing the rehabilitated horses had grown since last summer—creating more hours to Michael's days at the ranch.

Clay, too, had benefitted, finding he had great empathy for the damaged animals, needing someone to see their potential, to love them as-is, despite the scars of their past. He glanced at Michael and snorted. "Strong spirit, as you say, is a nice way of putting it. Where I grew up, we had a different term for that attitude."

Michael quietly continued to clean the hoof of the Appaloosa he'd just walked around the paddock. The old man, his silvery hair in one long braid down his back, nodded. "She can be prickly. I'll give you that. But she has a good heart, trust me. No one can handle troubled kids better than our Sally."

Clay picked up a pitchfork and started mucking stalls. "Too bad she hides it under that cactus of a personality."

Michael chuckled. "She was probably running late. She hates being late."

Promptness was something Clay prided himself on. He understood that. But the woman gave new meaning to the word tightly wrapped—and he was the one diagnosed with post-traumatic stress. He bit back a laugh at the sheer irony that he might have a greater patience level than the red-haired music teacher. "Chances are I didn't score any points with her." He shot a look at Michael whose steady gaze met his. "Not that I was trying."

The flutter of wings caught Clay's attention and he glanced up into the rafters just in time to see a Great White Owl swoop from the shadows and soar through the open door. He looked at Michael in amazement. "Did you see that?" He'd never been so close to a wild bird of that stature, where he could've reached out to touch the creature as it flew past.

Michael stood looking to where the owl had flown. He seemed unfazed by what Clay felt was a near miracle. "Must be a storm brewing." Michael scratched the back of his neck, his eyes landing on Clay.

As though hit by a cold punch, Clay held the old man's gaze. For the first time, he truly realized Michael's ethnic background. He sensed something spiritual, reverent in his eyes. Clay blinked, shook his head and passed his musing off as nonsense. "Well, I understand snow can happen without any warning in this neck of the woods."

Michael raised one silvery brow. "I don't know if this storm is about the weather. Storms come in many disguises."

Clay wasn't sure why Sally Andersen's face should pop into his brain. He shrugged off Michael's American Indian vibe and went back to work, stopping to listen to the low, mournful sound of the owl perched somewhere outside in the trees. He couldn't say what caused the hair to stand up on the back of his neck.

CHAPTER FIVE

Sally guided her horse into the stall, unaware that one of the boys from the trail ride had followed her inside. She'd noticed Clay at the other end of the barn, focused on adjusting something on his artificial leg, the denim pushed up over his knee. From the corner of her eye she noted Jarod skirting around her and running down to Clay, staring curiously at the mechanical leg. Sally looped the reins around the post and leaned out of the stall. "Jarod, please let's leave Mr. Saunders alone. He's a busy man."

Clay held up his hand and looked at her. He slid over on the wooden supply trunk he sat on and patted the seat next to him. "It's okay, Ms. Andersen. I've got a few minutes. What's your name, again? Mine's Clay." He held out his hand to the nine-year old.

"Jarod… sir." The boy looked from Sally to Clay's proffered hand. He accepted Clay's greeting and shook his hand. "Jarod Robins. I live with my mom down in Billings at Miss Ellie's house."

Clay nodded. "Yep, I know. Miss Ellie's good people. You do me a favor and make sure you watch out for your mom and Miss Ellie down there and I'll tell you anything you want to know about my leg. Deal?"

The boy gave an enthusiastic nod. "Sure thing." He eyed Clay's leg. "What happened? I mean, how'd you lose your leg?"

Sally set to brushing down her horse as she listened to Clay explain the ordeal in terms straightforward, but understandable for the boy's age.

"Does it hurt?" the boy asked.

Sally found her hand slowing as she listened. Eavesdropping wasn't her intent, but rather the boy asked questions that she'd wanted to ask had things between them not started as badly as they had. Even though he'd agreed to helping out with the auction, and he'd apologized, she couldn't explain how he seemed to intimidate her. She wasn't used to feeling that way about anyone, and it caused her more confusion than anything.

"It aches sometimes. Like when you get a bad headache, or a charlie horse in your foot," Clay answered.

"Is there stuff you can't do?"

"I'm not good at snowboarding," Clay laughed and the sound of it surprised Sally. She'd never heard him laugh—*ever*. She found herself smiling.

"Don't tell anyone, but I couldn't snowboard before I got hurt," Clay added conspiratorially "The thing is I've just had to retrain my body to compensate. And it's kind of cool, I've got one leg—this one—with a special boot, and another with a blade. I can run with that one, though I'm still getting used to it."

Sally peeked over the stable fence, spying on the two. Jarod looked up at Clay, focused on his every word.

"It's taken some getting used to, but I can pretty much do anything I did before, maybe just not as fast on my feet."

"That's cool. You're like a real hero. I see that on the news. So, do you have any medals?"

Sally smoothed her hand across the mare's silky mane, noticing how long of a pause had followed the question.

"Hey, you know what? I bet you Miss Ellie is waiting outside. You better hustle on out there. We'll talk more another time."

Sally leaned against the stall and waved at Jarod as he ran by. The grin on his face was a mile wide. Many of the kids and some of the women, by the time they reached Miss Ellie's "special house"—the term Ellie preferred over shelter—had never been outside the city. Most of her tenants had come there to get away from abusive situations—many of the kids had never known their real fathers. She was impressed with how patient and kind Clay had been with the curious young boy. "You really made his day," she said, walking down to where he'd started brushing down another horse. It was just the two of them in the barn. She'd run into Michael headed up to the main house to speak to Wyatt about a potential forever family adoption. Maybe it was how she'd treated him earlier. It was unfair, and the trail ride had given her time to think about it. But his kindness to Jarod made her poor behavior clearer. The waning sun cast long shadows inside the barn, glittering on the patches of snow dotting the ground outside. The mild temps of the day had given way to a chill, but the scent of straw and horses had a calming effect on Sally from the days in her youth when she'd ridden with Angelique out on her aunt's and uncle's ranch. That love of riding continued and had her life turned out differently, she would have loved to own a horse ranch of her own. She followed Clay's hand slid gently over the animals back. Once left for dead, the Appaloosa had been nursed back to health and brought to the ranch last fall. Under Michael's expert care, she was now less skittish around people. It occurred to her as she observed him that Clay, too had changed since they'd first met. She'd just never taken the time to notice.

"I don't know that I made his day, exactly," Clay answered finally, not looking up from his task. "But maybe I answered his questions." His response was short, gruff. She didn't blame him. She hadn't exactly been cordial to him, either. She hadn't thought it was a good idea to include him in the auction, and once chosen, instead of contacting him by phone, she'd let him find out on his own. Then again, she had a multitude of problems of her own, that few really, knew about. One of them had to do with the mandatory meeting Principal Kale had scheduled. She swallowed her pride and forged ahead, hoping to right at least one of her wrongs. "Listen, about earlier. I was admittedly…tense."

He continued grooming the horse. "You want to talk about it?" He didn't look up.

Sally looked at her dusty old worn-out boots, noting how akin her heart felt to them. How could she tell him that she felt like she was caught in a swirling sinkhole, being drawn closer and closer to losing it. Her job—the reason she'd been late—was called to discussion in an emergency meeting of the school board and Principal Kale as a result of the rumors concerning her promiscuous behavior in town. After the shock, feeling as though she'd been placed on public display she assured the members that the rumors were unfounded as most rumors are. The embarrassed members filed out and Principal Kale, while not issuing an apology, did say he was glad to hear the rumors weren't true. A remark Sally tucked away to remember come time when his position was up for renewal.

Sally toed the ground. There was more. She could have read Clay a litany of concerns. But he didn't know her, didn't understand that she'd used up nearly all of her inheritance for the unexpected costs of the renovation. It would be months, maybe years on her salary to rebuild it to the level where she could even consider having a child.

"Sally?"

She looked up, pulling from her reverie, realizing that Clay stood before her. He was studying her.

"Are you okay? You seemed to take off there for a few minutes."

She shook her head. "It's been a day—a long day." She waved off his query.

He tipped his head. "This have anything to do with those brochures?"

Her first inclination was to bolt. If another man so much as looked at her with that glimmer in his eye...

She glanced at him. No glimmer. Her shoulders slumped. She was tired of running from the topic, tired of trying to hide it. She pressed her lips tightly, her chin wobbling. Damn. It only hurt when she stopped to think about it. "I-It's n-nothing."

"Sally." His fingers touched her chin, forcing her gaze to his.

"Listen, I know we've had our differences, but you can talk to me. I'm not going to say anything to anyone. I've been through torture training. I can deal with a small town."

She smiled despite the fact that she felt like crying. Aimee had been the only person she'd felt she could talk to about this. Most men in town were more than ready, if rumors were true, to offer their services in bed. Clay hadn't. On most every level, in fact, they seem to mostly tolerate each other. He was a safe bet.

She sat down on the wood storage box and released a quiet sigh. "Have you ever looked around and felt like you're the only one who's different?" She hurried on. The idea that she could speak freely opened up the gates and she couldn't seem to get it out of her system fast enough. "All my friends are married, getting married, having kids," she said, ticking off each point on her fingers. "Some going on their second kid."

Clay eased down beside her, keeping his distance, and folded his hands over his knees as he listened. "You mean Wyatt and Aimee? They mentioned something about that at dinner the other day."

"Please understand, I am deliriously happy for them as I am for Rein and Liberty, and Dalton and Angelique." She looked up, eyeing the rafters. "And then there's Nate and Charlene, who are getting married and pretty soon I'll be hearing about their kids." She looked at him. "You know, all this never got to me before. I've been totally content with having my students each year. Starting out, I had my dad to care for and I thought I couldn't give any more than I already am." She shook her head. "Now I'm almost thirty-two and I know I'm not all that bad-looking, right?"

Clay glanced at her, surprise registered on his face. "Uh, no, I wouldn't say you're bad looking."

She held his gaze, deciding it best not to question him further. "I guess guys aren't drawn to me because—honestly, I don't know why." All the confusion, the questions about who she was and what she wanted out of life seemed to storm forward, desperate to be freed from her torment. "I realize there are some single guys around," she said with a chuckle. "Most who'd gladly hop in my bed in my quest to have a child, but wouldn't dream of going through the mundane things of asking a girl out, taking in a movie, making out in the back row—you know what I mean?"

Clay swiped his hand over his mouth and peered up at her with a narrowed look. "I think I'm following you. Just promise me there won't be a quiz at the end."

Sally snorted. This whole gossip wildfire incident had been a revelation. There were, apparently, men in town willing to bed her, but not marry her. And while at first, she'd found the idea playfully amusing—when she still had the luxury of her inheritance—it all seemed suddenly disheartening. Sally covered her face, unable to stop the dam of emotions breaking through. How had she gotten into this mess? Was she cursed to die alone with a houseful of cats running around her newly renovated home? The thought brought forth another anguished sob. She felt a weight around her shoulder and startled, looking up to see Clay's expression—a mix of surprise mixed with concern.

"Sally, it's going to be okay," he said softly. His gaze held hers.

She clung to his words, searched eyes that she hadn't noticed until now were really quite striking for the truth. Without thought, she wrapped her hand around his head and brought his lips to hers. Surprised as he no doubt was, she was desperate for the closeness, the intimacy. Her lips met his—akin to kissing a flat piece of wood.

This was a bad idea.

Until his hand curled around the back of her neck and his mouth came alive, capturing hers, effectively stopping all rational thought.

She moved her hand to his jaw, wanting to know the moment was real, brushing her fingertips across his unshaven cheek. Each time she thought the kiss was over, he'd capture her mouth again. Had they been anywhere else, there was little no doubt where this would most certainly lead.

"Miss Andersen? Mr. Saunders?" Emilee Kinnison's young voice severed the kiss, ending the intimacy. Sally had to catch herself from falling forward when Clay bolted to his feet.

Emilee skipped in, stopping short a few feet in the door. Sadie, the Kinnison brothers' first dog from their step-dad, trotted in at a slower pace, his tongue lolling from the side of his mouth. The little girl looked at Clay, then Sally. It had never been proven, but on more than one occasion, Emilee had indicated she had the gift, like her grandmother, of being a seer. To the Crow tribe, it was a gift passed on only to the females. Sally only hoped that whatever Emilee might have sensed was no more than PG-13.

The young girl beamed. "Grandma sent me down to tell you that supper is ready."

"Thank you, Em. Mr. Saunders was just telling me about his time overseas." She walked over and took the young girl's hand. "Come on, I'll race you back to the house." She glanced over her shoulder. "You coming, Mr. Saunders?"

She saw his jaw twitch. His smoky gaze indicated that kiss was anything but friendly.

"Be up in a bit," he answered.

The brisk run did little to quell the feelings Clay's kisses had stirred inside her. He'd seen the brochures, was most certainly aware of the rumors in town about her wanting a baby daddy. Maybe he was testing the waters for himself.

Later, as the entire Kinnison clan—including her, Clay, and Michael and Rebecca Greyfeather— sat around the massive, family table, Sally refused to make eye contact with Clay, and instead made small talk about the upcoming meeting at Betty's.

"We found tons of colored tissue paper when we went to Billings," Angelique offered. "We'll have plenty to make our giant tissue flowers."

Liberty pushed back from the table. "I hate to call it a night, but suddenly I'm barely able to keep my eyes open."

Rein was up from his chair, helping Liberty to where their coats hung in the foyer. Seated next to

Emilee, Sally noticed the young girl's concern. "Hey, Em, Liberty's going to be fine. Sometimes women who are going to have a baby get tired." She nudged the girl's shoulder. "Sometimes even when they aren't going to have a baby, women get tired." Sally winked at Emilee and finally received a smile.

"Goodnight all. I'll see you later in the week at Betty's," Liberty called as Rein ushered her out the door.

"Rebecca, let me help with the dishes," Sally offered.

Michael and Wyatt stood to help.

"I'll get this. You all go relax. Tell Aimee to put her feet up." She hadn't the nerve to look at Clay, though a few times during the evening, she'd sensed him looking at her.

"Well, early day tomorrow. Think I'll turn in." Clay stood. "Thank you, Rebecca. As always, your meals are amazing." He smiled and waved at the small group beginning to settle in front of the fire. It was then that he tossed Sally a quick nod. "Miss Andersen." He grabbed his ball cap from the deer antler hat rack in the foyer and was gone.

Sally collected the leftover food and carried it to the kitchen. Starting the search for containers to put them in. Lost in the task, she looked up and met Rebecca's gaze across the kitchen table.

Emilee, who'd finished with bringing in the plates for her grandmother, giggled as she trotted out of the room to play with Sadie.

"Do I look odd?" Sally asked the woman whom she'd known as a second mother most of her young life.

Rebecca went about the work of loading the dishwasher. "No, why do you ask?" She glanced over her shoulder with a motherly smile.

"Maybe because you and your grand-daughter keep looking at me like you're seeing something I don't." Sally snapped the lid on the container and tucked it in the refrigerator. Secured with flower-shaped magnets to the front door of the appliance were pictures taken over the past year—Wyatt riding with Aimee his new bride into the sunset, a photo of the Kinnisons around a massive Christmas tree, a tradition that had been absent far too many years in the house until Aimee came along. There was a picture of Dalton, Rein, Hank, and Clay at the old hunting cabin on a fall weekend fishing trip. Her gaze lingered on Clay, grinning with a fishing pole in one hand, a beer in the other. "Anything you care to share with me?" Sally asked turning to Rebecca. "Anything I should know?" She crossed her arms over her chest and waited.

The older woman was the picture of aging with grace. She'd always possessed an air of wisdom. Her dark eyes shone even now with it. "Seers aren't astrologists, Sally. Sometimes things remain shadowed until they are meant to be seen."

Sally had seen both Rebecca and her granddaughter's skills at work in other people's lives, but they'd never before been directed toward her. While she had great respect for the gift and for the vessels, she wasn't sure yet that she believed—or even wanted to, now that the cosmic light seemed to be shining down on her.

"Well, you let me know if something becomes clear." Sally crooked her fingers for emphasis. This had been the single strangest week of her adult life, and what had happened tonight in the barn was icing on that crazy cake. "I'm going to scoot on down to my cabin, if you don't need me up here for anything. Thank you and please, I'd love to get your pot roast recipe from you sometime."

"All you really need is a good slow-cooker," Rebecca smiled as she resumed her task.

"All right, then. Good night." Sally got as far as the kitchen door.

"Sally?"

She looked over her shoulder.

"He's not like the others." Rebecca regarded her for a moment, then went back to her dishes.

And with that, Sally headed to her cabin and a sleepless night of trying to decipher between that kiss and what Rebecca's insight meant.

It'd taken him a few minutes to compose himself before he could show up at dinner after that kiss. Not just from the painful tightening in his jeans, but emotionally. And that night—thinking about it maybe a hundred or so times, in conjunction with a lusty fantasy of what might have happened had they found a dark corner on a soft bed of clean straw— well, let's just say his dick hadn't seen that kind of action in a very long time.

Clay, was in many ways, relieved when renovations were finally complete and Sally was able to return home. Delighted with her joy at the remodel, Rein had tried to wave off her paying for the labor, but she fought him, insisting on paying him what they'd agreed on.

Clay was just glad not to have her a few yards away, seeing her every morning, and forced to pretend as though nothing had happened between them each time their paths crossed.

Finishing up for the evening on a project at Rein's house, Clay decided to stop in at Betty's and grab a burger to go. He was too tired to fix anything and just wanted to get back to a hot shower and his unmade bed.

The minute he walked into Betty's to pick up his dinner, he realized what day it was. There, in a separate room used for special parties sat Sally and her Buckle Ball entourage. Laughter filtered out over the scant number of visitors on the chilly Tuesday evening. From what he could tell, it appeared they were having a great time.

"Hey, Clay. How are you this evening?" Betty met him at the register located at the end of the old soda fountain counter with its eight chrome-and-red leather ice cream stools. "Jerry's just about got your order ready. Why don't you take a load off, and I'll get you a cup of fresh coffee while you wait?"

"Thanks, Betty." Clay sat down on the first stool nearest the door. He had no desire to see Sally. He'd had a hard enough time trying to put behind the lingering smoke of that fiery kiss they'd shared.

Betty set a cup in front of him. She glanced toward the room. "Those girls have been laughing like that since they sat down. Like a bunch of schoolgirls." She smiled. "Like to hear laughter like that once in a while—does a heart good, you know?" She eyed the group. "Still, can't help wanting to be a fly on the wall to cause such a ruckus."

Clay nodded and took a sip of his coffee. Nope, he had no desire to know what they might be talking about. He peered over his cup at Jerry standing at the stove in the kitchen. They'd never put a door between the kitchen and customers. Jerry wanted folks to feel at home, wanted the smell of food to lure people in. He was busy at work, putting together the café's famous special cheeseburger with bacon and cheese that he'd ordered.

"What have you been up to?" Betty asked, swiping vintage malt glasses with a dry towel and setting them in her special display cabinet above the malt machine.

"Got in a few more horses at the ranch this morning. Sent one out to live with a good family. We'll check on them, make sure things are going well. But it looked really promising." He sighed and rubbed one eye. "I've been helping Rein up at his place, helping him finish that basement project."

"Oh, yes, Liberty mentioned you boys were working on that tonight," Betty said over her shoulder. "Making it into a family room?"

Clay nodded. "Family room, guest room that walks out to the patio. They wanted to get it ready for times when they have family and friends over."

Betty smiled. "Those boys have been through a lot, and Liberty, too, for that matter. Rein losing his parents when he was just a kid, and poor Liberty." She tossed down her hand towel. "I'm just glad she had the good sense to get away from that poor excuse of a father."

"You got any kids, Betty?" Clay had never seen any pictures behind the counter. Never heard her talk about her own kids, always somebody else's kids.

She cleared her throat and after a moment looked at him, her eyes shimmered with unshed tears. "Nope, wasn't able to carry them to term. A glitch in my body, I guess. But my sis has got seven kids. We're real close to all seven, God-parents to the oldest four."

Clay smiled at the vivacious, friendly woman that seemed a mother figure to almost everyone in town. "You've got a heart as big as Texas, Betty, and I should know since I was raised there."

"No kidding? Jerry and I once drove all the way down there to compete in a chili-cooking contest. Winner received ten-thousand dollars toward his restaurant and the recipe in some fancy cookbook."

"Really? Did you win?"

Betty laughed. "Heck, no. but we had a great time sampling the food between here and there."

"Clay!"

He turned to see Aimee waving him over. "Come here and give us your opinion."

Clay grinned and held up his hand. "I'm no good at decorations."

"Yes, but you are one of our esteemed bachelors for the auction and since this will be displayed around the stage, that makes your thoughts valuable."

Clay glanced at Betty, who nudged him to go with a nod.

"I'll bring out your food when its ready."

"Evenin' ladies," he might have let his southern drawl slip out in the greeting. He stood in the wide arched entrance to the room. Liberty, Ellie, Aimee,

Angelique, Kaylee, and Sally sat around the large farmhouse table. Rainbow colored squares of tissue paper littered the surface.

"Hey, Mr. Spring Buckle Ball bachelor." Ellie said with a smile. "Say that ten times really quick." She said, nudging Angelique beside her. "Are you prepared to have hundreds of single women fighting over you—figuratively speaking, of course?" Ellie looked around the table. "This auction thing doesn't get ugly, does it?"

Aimee shook her head and took another bite of what looked to be a mile-high meringue on a slice of coconut cream pie. She closed her eyes, bliss etched on her face. "This little one loves coconut cream pie. What do you suppose that means?"

Clay hadn't given much thought to the date aspect of the auction, or who he'd end up with. He'd been focused on too many other things of late. He glanced at Sally, quickly looking away. "Well, I can't speak for what might happen, but I'm honored to be part of such a good cause."

Ellie smiled. "You are a darling young man, and if I were younger I'd be saving my pennies to snag you for myself." She blew him a quick kiss.

"Well, you can bet I've been saving *my* pennies," Kaylee stated, tossing another completed flower into the corner.

Clay hoped that she was saving them for Tyler. Poor guy hadn't stopped talking about Kaylee since he first saw her. "Ladies, it looks like you're off to a great start. I've got to check on my dinner. Have fun." He turned, and Betty, her face washed in fear, ran into him, grabbing his arms.

"It's Jerry, something's wrong. H-he's n-not moving."

Clay moved around her and hurried to the kitchen. Jerry lay on the floor. He was out cold.

Betty followed. "I heard him call my name, and by the time I reached him, he was on his knees, speaking… but I couldn't understand a word he was saying."

Clay knelt down and did a quick physical assessment, his combat training kicking in instinctively. He noted the distorted features of one side of the man's face. A gash, likely from the fall, bled from his forehead. He found a pulse and looked up. "Someone call 911."

Aimee held up her phone. "Got it." She stepped away to make the call.

"Sally, get everyone out of here. We need to make room for the paramedics." The Emergency Medical Unit resided in the firehouse. Only two medics comprised the EMT staff, and they served all the tiny mountain towns in the area. Clay prayed they were close by.

Betty grabbed a wad of hand towels and gently tucked them beneath Jerry's head. She looked over her shoulder. "Sally, Liberty, would you girls take care of things out front? Take care of the customers, tell them we need to close early."

Liberty touched Betty's shoulder. "We'll take care of things here. Don't worry."

When it was just her and Clay, she looked at him. Her vivid blue eyes, normally alive with joy, were filled with concern.

"What happened?" she asked.

"He has a pulse, Betty, and he's breathing. It looks like he bumped his head in the fall—maybe the stove handle." He covered Betty's hand, resting now on her husband's chest. He couldn't be sure, not until the medics had a chance to look at him, but his best guess was that Jerry had suffered a stroke.

The blue and red flashing lights of the Medivac truck flickered through the front windows.

Clay stood and draped his arm around Betty's shoulders as the medics worked on Jerry. They placed him on oxygen, got him on a gurney and wheeled him outside, choosing instead to go through the alley door. "You go on with Jerry. We'll lock up."

Betty grabbed her purse and coat. She looked at Clay and then scanned the kitchen as though unsure whether to leave.

He took her by the shoulders. "Don't worry. We've got this. It'll be fine."

She hadn't shed a single tear. Shock still held her emotions at bay.

Angelique appeared and took Betty's hand. "Come on, we'll follow the ambulance to Billings."

Betty nodded and grabbed Clay's hand in a fierce grip. "Thank you."

He stood at the alley door and watched the ambulance take off with Angelique and Betty close behind. It dawned on him that the stove was probably still on and drawing a deep breath to calm his racing heart, he locked the back door and set to the task of shutting down, and cleaning up the kitchen.

In the main room, Sally and Liberty had taken care of the customers, locking the door behind them and were bussing the tables. The rest of the group was busy gathering up the flowers and bagging their completed work.

Sally walked into the kitchen carrying a gray tub full of dirty dishes. "Put these in the dishwasher, wipe down the tables, refill the napkin dispensers, check the salt and pepper shakers."

"Sally," Clay said listening to her ramble under her breath.

"Put the pies in the refrigerator." She stood with her hands braced on the sink. "Count the till...drop it at the bank."

He wasn't sure if she was talking to him, or checking off a mental list.

"Sally," he said a little louder, hoping to shake her from her reverie. He'd seen many different ways that people handled trauma and stress—hell, he was no poster child for calm, that much was true. But twice now, he'd seen her unravel before his eyes. She turned suddenly to face him. Given the look on her face, he wasn't sure whether to duck or run.

"Why does shit like this always seem to happen to good people?" Her shoulders slumped as she shook her head. "Betty and Jerry are two of the nicest people I know. They're always doing something for this community."

Clay listened, something he'd done a lot around Sally Andersen of late—besides kissing her. "He's going to be okay. It might be a while before he recovers fully though."

She shot a laser-like gaze to his. "What do you mean? Did the medics say what happened?"

"No," He went back to scrubbing the stove. "But I know what a stroke looks like."

"A stroke?" Sally pushed her palm to her forehead. She glanced at Clay. "You know it's Betty who comes up with the ideas, but it's Jerry who's the real cook. He's the one who puts out the food. Well, except of course Rebecca's pies and pastries."

Aimee stuck her head inside the door. "What else can we do?"

Sally tucked her arm through Aimee's. "Come on, Liberty and I can show you. You know that I used to work here as a waitress back in high school." She stopped suddenly. "Wow, that was a long time ago."

They walked out and Clay was grateful to have the kitchen to himself. He glanced at the sack on the serving shelf, realizing it was likely his supper. After popping it in the microwave to heat it through, he sat down on an old wooden stool at the prep table and dissected the burger, eyeing its content, tasting the simple spices of garlic, salt, pepper, and something he couldn't quite detect. Hungrier than he thought, he finished the second burger, making note of how Jerry had put it together. Licking his lips, he sat back with a satisfied sigh. Damn, if it wasn't one of the best burgers he'd ever tasted. He scanned the L-shaped backroom—it had a walk-in freezer tucked in one corner, surrounded on the remaining walls by floor-to-ceiling pantry shelves filled with dry goods and canned staples. A stainless-steel island separated the longer portion of the room in half, dividing the stove from shelves of dishware and serving pieces. Jerry had an extensive alphabetized spice wall rack within arm's reach of the stove. "I could do this," he said quietly as he shifted on the stool to take in the entire kitchen set-up. He'd have to run it past Betty, of course, and Rein. He didn't realize that he wasn't alone.

"Do what?" Sally asked, walking past him, her arms loaded with an arsenal of condiment bottles.

Clay used a napkin to wipe his fingers and mouth. "Fill in for Jerry, at least temporarily, until Betty finds someone else." He took his plate to the dishwasher, aware that as he did, it placed a greater distance between him and Sally. That was probably a good thing.

"You can cook?"

Clay tossed her a lingering look, observing how efficiently she'd lined up the bottles to refill them. "I took a couple of classes in college. I've always messed around in the kitchen."

"Messed around?" She chuckled softly. The sound of it washed a little too well over his tired mind just now.

He shrugged, choosing to stay focused and not allow the conversation to drift into dangerous waters—like discussing that night in the barn. "I used to watch my mom in the kitchen. She was a great cook. My dad wasn't around much— workaholic, so I learned how to cook meals so it'd be ready for mom when she got home from work."

He'd been so busy loading the dishwasher that it took him a moment to realize she hadn't responded. He glanced back, expecting to find himself alone. Instead, he found her standing behind him. She had her arms folded across her chest, the grey Mickey Mouse T-shirt and those faded jeans looking every bit as sexy to him as peek-a-boo lingerie. He cleared his throat, letting those thoughts dissolve. "What is it? What'd I say? You've got that look that teachers give you when it seems they're trying to dissect your brain."

"No." She smiled, eyeing him. "It's you. Everything you say, everything you do. It's like you're not the same person who came here less than a year ago."

Clay's brows rose. He hadn't expected that. "I suppose it's been good for me. The Last Hope Ranch has lived up to its name as far as I'm concerned. The hard work, being around my old college buddies, working with Michael and the horses—"

"I want to have a baby." Her gaze was steady.

He'd tiptoed his way through a minefield or two in his time—he could handle this. He reached for a towel and wiped his hands, proceeding cautiously. "Yeah, I saw the brochures." He glanced over her shoulder and saw the rest of the ladies seated in the other room, busy talking.

"No, what I mean is…I really hadn't given this much thought—you know, about asking somebody to help me." She looked away as though piecing it together in her brain. "I could pay you a fee, of course, and there would have to be some legal issue—a contract.

Whoa. Contract? Clay suddenly felt the need for a drink. He opened one cabinet and then another. Surely Jerry kept a stash of whiskey around, if only for cooking.

"What are you doing?" she asked.

"Looking for the whiskey."

"Jerry's a beer drinker," Sally answered.

"That'll do." He continued to check every cabinet and shelf in the kitchen.

"You think I'm crazy."

It wasn't really a question. More of a statement of fact as presented—he just happened to agree. "Bingo." He leveled her a look, then went back to his quest.

She walked toward him and he had the strongest urge to grab a rolling pin. But a greater battle roiled inside him. His libido was on fire, ready to sign on the dotted line, but common sense cautioned him to keep his dick as far from her as possible.

"Look, it's not like I'm asking you to commit to anything." She scooted her fine little ass on the wooden stool and crossed her legs. "You know; it was really that kiss that got me to consider this idea."

Good to know she'd been affected. Crazy train wasn't exactly the response he'd planned on.

"It's perfect," she continued. "You have no ties here. I assume you're not planning on staying since your only family is out in California."

Clay stared at her, trying to decide if the woman was certifiable or simply delusional. Did he look like the kind of guy who could walk away from his own child? "You don't know anything about me."

Her face lit up. "I know, that's why it's perfect. I don't really need to know much. I already know you're kind to animals, patient with kids, you're a hard worker, former military, good in medical emergencies, and you can cook." She lifted her palms. "What more, other than your health, do I need to know?" She eyed him. "And from here you look pretty damn healthy."

Clay blinked, waiting for his brain to catch up with his good sense, which kept tripping on his libido. He felt like a damn racehorse, and if she asked him to smile— "Look, Sally. I'm flattered, really. But they have places—clinics—I'm sure they're mentioned in the brochures. Places where guys can donate—"

"Sperm, Clay," she interjected. "And yes, I know. I've done the research. Crunched the numbers. And honestly, the bottom line looks grim. My insurance covers only the initial exams and tests. The rest of it I would be financially responsible for." She held his eyes for a moment more, then slapped her hand on the table. "You know, you're right. It's a crazy idea." She hopped off the stool. "Forget I mentioned it."

Later that night as he lay staring at his bedroom ceiling he decided that when it came to Sally Andersen, he had a lot to try to forget. First, was the kiss that jumpstarted his motor in a way he hadn't felt in way too long, and now this…*proposition*. Both difficult to shove aside, especially given that he hadn't had sex in well over a year since he'd been at the ranch.

"I don't need to know anything, really."

Her words played over and over in his brain. Looking down, he lifted his stump of a leg and wondered how she'd feel about being in bed with that. He hadn't given a second thought to how his fiancée would react. They'd been madly in love before he deployed, active sexually, and on more than one occasion had phone sex while he was overseas. He'd been more focused on adjusting to his new condition than considering what she might want or need. He'd mistakenly assumed she'd be there for him, no matter what. Hell, everything else, thankfully, was fully operational. As it turned out, she couldn't make the adjustment. It was a blow, one that came on the heels of his mother's stroke that ultimately evolved into Alzheimer's.

He pushed his hands over his face, mentally washing off the residual pain of the look on his fiancée's face as she left him. He shook his head to clear it, pulling his thoughts back to the present. All the woman really wanted was his swimmers. Maybe she wouldn't care. Maybe she wouldn't notice his partial leg, or the deep scars that marred his skin from shrapnel. Simple mechanics. Insert tab A into slot B. What guy wouldn't jump at the chance for unbridled, commitment-free sex? No strings attached. The very idea semi-aroused him. Was he insane to even give this ridiculous plan of hers a second thought? She was right. He hadn't planned on making his life here. His only family lived on the coast and thanks to X-box, he and his nephews had found common ground. Besides, he'd probably be gone before she had the baby.

And right there is where his common sense caught up and put an abrupt halt to the lusty, whirlwind of thoughts. He sat up, battling with the question rolling around in his brain. *Was she serious?*

There was really only one way to know for sure. Even as he secured his leg and tried to tell himself he only wanted to talk, talking was the last thing he had on his mind.

CHAPTER SIX

"They've admitted Jerry for more tests, but the initial assessment appears to be a stroke. The severity is what they've yet to determine."

"And Betty? How's she holding up?" Sally asked.

"About as you'd expect. The woman is tough, but she looks tired. I know she was grateful that you all took care of things for her. That was a big weight off her shoulders. But she is going to keep the café closed for a couple of days, so she can be here."

"Be sure to give her and Jerry my love. What about you? Are you heading home?"

"I'll be sure to tell her. Actually, Dalton and Em are on their way down to pick me up. Betty wants to stay, so I'm leaving her my car."

The threat of tears pricked at Sally's eyes. Despite the frequent annoyances of living in a small town, there were moments—like these—when she cherished this dinky little place. "You guys drive safely and I'll talk to you tomorrow. Thank you for the update."

Sally stood for a moment in the quiet house. Marriage. Longevity. Her parents' divorce. She thought of how many years Betty and Jerry had been together—all they'd weathered together over the years. It gave her pause to think about raising a child alone. There would be plenty of opinions, either way—that much she knew was true. There was a time, sure, that she'd waited patiently for her cowboy to sweep her off her feet and ride her into the sunset, but weeks turned to months, months to years and after waiting, after the dead-end dates, she'd made the decision that her happiness was not reliant on having a man in her life. She found fulfilment in her profession, working with kids, had trusted friends, and relative financial security. A child of her own, one created in her body, brought into this world by her, raised by her with her love, became her heart's single desire. She wasn't the type to overthink things. Once an idea presented itself, she'd research it to near obsession, and if no flaws, no deterrents were found, she'd proceed as planned. So it had been with wanting a baby. It was bringing the world around to her plan that was her greatest obstacle.

She eased into her grandmother's rocking chair and pulled the afghan kept there around her shoulders. The view from the tiny Victorian gothic turret on the second floor gave a view of the quiet street and of the gravel drive and old garage at the side of the house. An old pine stood tall between the back door and the garage, its branches reaching out as though shading the falling apart one-car garage that was in desperate need of repair. When young, she used to sit in the little space off her bedroom and read or play with her dolls. Like many a young girl, she always assumed that there'd be a 'Ken' for her as well one day. But those dreams had faded with time.

"You think I'm crazy." Her words came back to haunt her. His felt much worse.

"Bingo."

She glanced around the room, seeing the stark changes before her, remembering when she'd stripped down the old lavender gingham checked curtains given the majority of her stuffed animals and dolls to those who could use them. Over time, when she had the money, she'd worked on stripping old flowered wallpaper and painting, polishing the beautiful hardwood floor and finding soft tufted areas rugs to sink into after a hard day.

She'd transformed the room, with its calming seas colors and shabby chic rustic décor, in a place of serenity—her little respite from the world. Over the years she'd added items she'd carefully selected from flea markets and antique stores. Her greatest splurge, before the renovations, was a bed set ordered from a hotel chain where she'd stayed during a teacher's conference in Kansas City.

But this change was far different than anything she'd ever tackled. Her biological clock was ticking. It was true that women were often getting married and having children much later than the generation before. Having to watch her father deteriorate and so rapidly in a few years only fueled her resolve to be young enough to enjoy this child while her health was good. She dropped the blanket over the back of the chair, and tucked her shoes under the old wooden bench at the end of her bed. She slipped into her T-shirt and baggy pajama bottoms with faded hearts, brushed her teeth, and lowered the speed of the ceiling fan she preferred to overhead lighting.

Crawling beneath the thick comforter and clean sheets she'd taken from the dryer this morning, she switched off her bedside lamp and watched the ceiling blades spin lazily, until she could no longer keep her eyes open.

Sally didn't want to wake up. An insistent noise had interrupted the fabulously sexy dream she'd been having with a faceless man. The sound pulled her awake and she turned her head to note the time. Uncertain if she were still asleep, she pushed up wearily on her elbow and squinted at the old alarm clock. *Did that say two o'clock?*

She fumbled for her cell phone and through blurry eyes searched for messages and missed calls. Much to her relief, there were none since Angelique's last update. Another round of knocks, louder this time, brought her fully alert. She swung her legs over the bed and flipped on the bedside lamp. This was no dream. Someone was at the door. She grabbed her hoodie, struggling with the zipper as she navigated the stairs in the dark, chiding herself for not turning on the light.

As she reached the bottom step, she flipped on the porch light. Comforted that Rein had suggested the dead bolt and had put one on both the front and back doors, she peeked out of the lace curtain covering the narrow beveled window along the side of the front door. Standing on her porch, his hand braced against her door, was Clay Saunders.

He glanced up, catching her gaze just before she stepped back. Her hand over her chest, Sally stood a moment trying to quell the sudden racing of her heart.

"Let me in, Sally." His voice, low and steady, came through the two-inch thick, wooden door.

She swallowed, wondering if he'd closed down Dusty's after leaving the restaurant. "Have you been drinking?" she asked, leaning against the door.

"Not a drop. Open up, we need to talk," he said in response.

Chewing her lip, she debated the wisdom of opening the door—in particular, since she was fairly sure the faceless man in her sexy dream had been Clay.

"Sally, it's damn cold out here," he said. The screen door squeaked open.

She released a deep breath, turned the deadbolt, unlocked the door, and stepped away as he pushed his way around the door.

"Shut the door," he ordered, taking off his gloves and unzipping his coat. He hung his jacket beside hers on the shabby chic coat hanger she'd gotten last week on a whim at deep discount. The contrast between coats was intriguing, but not nearly as much as why he was standing in her foyer at two in the morning. He looked around and rubbed his hands together.

She pulled her gaze to his.

"Did you really mean what you said tonight?"

Oh, shit. Sally swallowed and held his steady gaze. She'd been right. He'd rolled out of bed, tossed a T-shirt and jeans on and drove all the way into town—just to ask her if she'd been serious. "You mean the thing… about the p-proposition?"

He kept his eyes to hers as he reached out and bolted the door. "Yeah. The proposition."

She darted a glance at the door. It wasn't fear that caused her heart to feel like a thundering herd of wild horses. "What are you doing?" His eyes held hers as he closed the gap between them.

"Practicing. Auditioning." He cupped her face with his hands. "Whatever you want to call it. Sorry, my hands are still cold."

She hadn't noticed. Her temperature was already on the rise given that dream she'd been having. Sally shut her eyes. His fingertips brushed across her cheek, slipping down the side of her neck, leaving a trail of fire in their wake. Opening her eyes, she met his just inches from hers. *Was this going to happen?*

"I'm going to kiss you," he stated lowering his mouth within a breath of hers. "Is that okay?"

"S-sure, okay." She heard the word, but focused on memory of his kiss, of how he tasted—how his tongue had teased, wanting surrender.

"We'll see how things go from there, agreed?" he whispered, his breath fanning her face as his lips brushed over hers.

She succumbed to his soft seduction, clinging to the hem of his shirt to steady herself when her knees felt like buckling. "I don't have any paperwork," she said quietly, though she couldn't have cared less. It had been a very long time since a man had seduced her.

"Just a trial run." He kissed her then, full on lip-lock. Sally's brain went into shutdown, while her girl parts all but trembled with anticipation. She grabbed the back of his head, holding his face to hers, giving back the hunger in his kisses. A basket fell as he backed her against the wall. Heat ignited between them. Sally wanted to see him, touch his skin bronzed by the sun. She wanted his hands all over her. "Clay," she spoke breathlessly between kisses, "I'm not sure this is wise. I don't have protection."

He captured her mouth again, even as he unzipped her hoodie, unceremoniously dragging it from her shoulders and tossing it over the stair railing. "If it comes to that, I've got it covered."

Surprised when he lifted her, she hooked her legs around his waist as he carried her to the couch in the front room. He perched her on the arm of the chair and held his arms up as she tugged the shirt over his head. Good lord. She touched him, delighted to feel him shudder. Moving her hands over the hard muscled plane of his chest, she stood ready to show him to her room. He stopped her.

"Tell me what you want, Sally." His eyes searched hers.

"You, Clay." She took his hand and he held her in place.

"You're sure?"

She had no hesitation. "Yes, I'm sure."

"Okay, but tonight we do things my way." He tugged her back to the couch.

He sat her on the chair arm, and kissed her, his hands meanwhile slipping her pajama bottoms down her hips. She clung to the couch as he slid them off and tossed them aside.

"You're so damn beautiful." He took her face, tilting it up to meet his. His kiss was slow, thorough, drugging her senses.

"I knew when I slept here that night this would be perfect," he whispered, nibbling her ear lobe.

"Oh?" was all she could answer, delightfully lost in the wonder of his kisses. "Perfect?"

His hand cradled the small of her back as he tipped her back on the couch. He braced one hand as he bent down to kiss one breast and then the other. His calloused hands moved down her body, parting her knees, his fingers skimming her sensitive flesh.

"I'm not sure what to do." She looked up at him from the odd angle.

"Enjoy." He leaned down, brushing his shadowy jaw to the soft flesh of her inner thigh.

"Oh lord," she sighed, reaching out tentatively to touch the top of his head.

He chuckled low. "Relax, Sally, I got this."

She dug her fingers into the couch cushion, surrendering to her sensations, floating between bliss and reality. Control slipped away. It'd been so long…so very long since she'd allowed herself such freedom. "Clay," she whispered. He continued, relentless, drawing her to a blind euphoria. At last, digging her heels into the couch, she came apart in a shattering climax.

He leaned over and pressed his lips to her navel.

She lay listless—divinely—astounded by his prowess, by how easily she'd given him control. As she tried to catch her breath, she opened her eyes and found him standing at the end of the couch holding his hands out to help her up. "Wait. Are we done? Is that it?" God, she felt sexy, freed from inhibition. This was new and intoxicating.

He pulled her upright, took her face in his hands and kissed her thoroughly. "I hope we're just getting started, Sally. That's up to you."

"But you haven't touched me, I mean…"

"With my dick? Yeah, I know. I think we should leave it at that for tonight."

"Are you serious?" she asked, still reeling from the most amazing thing she'd experienced since post-it notes.

He held out her clothes and kissed her on the forehead. "I had to know if you were serious and," he shrugged, "if we had chemistry."

"Does there need to be?" she asked tugging on her pajamas, though it was the last thing she truly wanted.

"I'm not a machine, Sally." He studied her. "And I won't lie to you. As much as we both think it's wise to keep emotions out of this arrangement, I warn you it could get complicated."

Sally watched as he pulled his shirt back on. She hadn't expected the war of emotions occurring inside her. For the first time, she questioned not Clay, but herself, in keeping things in check. She nodded. "I didn't think it would be easy. I guess that's why I thought you were the perfect candidate. I have no past with you, no future."

He held her gaze a moment longer, then nodded. "I should go. Don't want neighbors seeing my truck parked out front."

"Oh, right." She hugged her arms as she followed him to the door where he slipped on his coat.

"Uh, Clay. About the bachelor auction coming up."

He nodded, righting the umbrella stand, and faced her.

"For… well, lots of reasons, really, I think it'd be best, that is if you're agreeing to this, if you weren't with,"—she crooked her fingers for emphasis—"other women during the term of our contract."

He glanced away as if in thought, then met her gaze. "Does that apply to you, as well?"

"Of course." She grabbed her hoodie and slipped it over her chilled arms. "Also, just so you're aware, I plan to bid on you at the auction."

He frowned. "I figured I would drop the auction. Come up with some reason."

"No, we can't do that. It'd send up a red flag."

"And you don't need any more rumors." He blew out a sigh and pulled his knit cap down over his ears. "Okay, you let me know when you have the papers ready." He looked at her and she could see the heat smoldering in those dark orbs. "Get some sleep." And with that he was gone.

Sally stared at the door and folded her arms over her still-tingling breasts. She had to remember that this had to do with an agreement and nothing more. No secondary emotions of possessiveness, wanting to cuddle, having breakfast and laughing over the Sunday comics. She was hiring him to perform a task—do a job. Her heart raced in anticipation of their next meeting and what skills she had yet to experience. *Sleep?* "Not likely," she muttered to herself.

Clay hadn't heard from Sally. It'd been over a week since the last time he'd had a good night's sleep, his mind unable to forget the sexy fantasy they'd shared. Maybe she'd changed her mind. It'd probably be in her best interest if she did. God, he hoped she hadn't.

It was three days until the auction. He had to admit he was more than a little nervous. They agreed to be monogamous and there was little required of the bachelors other than to escort the winner to the dance and the remainder of the evening. They'd never really finalized the idea that she'd bid on him. He could very well wind up with one of the nursing home blue hairs. That thought led back to Betty's call earlier in the day. She'd called to give him an update. "I wanted to thank you and the girls for taking care of things the other night. They've released Jerry to the nursing home up here in town and then he'll have some home health care therapy after he comes home. He's going to be okay I think, but it will be awhile before he's able to work at the café."

"Yeah, Betty, about that," Clay started. "Listen, things are slow around here right now and if Rein can schedule his remodel around it, I thought I'd offer to step in as your cook. Just until you find a better replacement. I'm pretty decent around the kitchen."

"Clay Saunders, you are a God-send. An angel sent to this earth."

"Uh, Betty, I'm not Wolfgang Puck, but I can do comfort food." Clay was warmed just the same by the woman's appreciation.

"You've no idea how much pressure it takes off me right now. I haven't had the chance to talk with Jerry about the future. I was waiting to see how well he responds to his therapy."

"And that's exactly where his focus needs to be right now, Betty. Trust me on this. I'm more than happy to help. When do you need me?"

"Tomorrow, six a.m.?"

He wasn't at all surprised she'd be anxious to get the café back open after being closed for almost a week. "Let me work out my schedule, Betty. But I'll be in as soon as I can."

"Thank you, Clay. Angelique has also offered also to come in and help with prep work."

He heard a sniff on the other end of the line. "Don't worry, Betty. It'll all work out. You tell Jerry to take care and don't give the nurses grief."

"I will. Thank you, Clay," she replied. "A wonderful God-send," she said quietly.

Hours later, he leaned back on his couch, tossed his game controller aside, and took a sip of a homemade brew that Dalton had been testing. His cell phone rang, and he had to shift aside a pile of newspapers and mail to find it. It was his sis, Julie, calling from California. He glanced at the clock on the fireplace mantel. Ten-thirty, which made it around nine-thirty her time. He'd just signed off with his nephews not more than an hour ago. "Hey, Jules, everything okay?" It wasn't like her to call at random in the middle of the week like this. Her calls, rare at that, were generally Sunday afternoons.

"Hi, Clay, did I catch you at a bad time?"

Clay noted the weariness in her voice. "Just got done playing a game with the boys. They're getting too damn good, you know. Probably ought to watch who they play with online."

She chuckled, though it wasn't with her usual heart. "Yeah, I'll get right on that." There was a brief silence. "Actually, it's about the boys that I called."

"They giving you a hard time? Really, Jules, if playing games is causing problems with their homework or other friends then—"

"It's not them, Clay. Or you."

He released a quiet sigh of relief. It had been when he'd visited over Christmas that he learned of the boy's interest—as most their age—in gaming. Clay had gotten the latest system shortly after he moved into the cabin at the Last Hope ranch. It'd served as an escape at the time, from the realities he'd seen. Every shot he fired on the animated screen was another of the bastards that had killed his friends and left him alone to carry the memory.

"I called because the boys have a spring break coming up soon, and I thought maybe they could come visit you, if you didn't mind," Julie asked.

"I'd love that, Jules. You know, there are more than enough empty cabins here right now. You could all come out. Get Louis on a horse. I'd love to see that." Clay grinned, but his gut told him something wasn't right.

"Yeah, well. You know Louis. He wouldn't dare want to scuff up his Gucci's."

Clay smiled, choosing not to respond with what he thought about his brother-in-law's lack of interest in anything but himself. "When is break?" he asked.

She sighed. It was uncharacteristic of her. She'd always been a take-charge kind of woman. A really good mom, as it turned out. Once Clay was able to see past his own issues. "Jules, what's going on? That's like the third time you've sighed since we've been talking. Are you feeling okay?" He sat upright, leaning his elbows on his knees as he listened.

Her heard her swallow. "I'm fine. Things are…fine. I just think Louis and I could use some time alone. Maybe go somewhere—the beach. He used to love the beach," she said as though an afterthought.

Clay had noticed her husband's absence even over the holiday season. He'd hoped that it had been end-of-the-year deadlines. He was beginning to sense there was more to this story. "Well, listen, if the boys want to come out, I'd love to have them here. They can stay here in the cabin. It's got a second room. They can help me out around the ranch. Maybe learn to ride."

"That sounds amazing, Clay, thank you."

"You're welcome to visit, too, Jules, anytime," Clay added. "I have a feeling you'd love this place. Kind of reminds me of Texas. End of the Line, the little town up the road from here, is pretty low-key, much the same as Piedmont was. You remember?"

He could hear the smile in her voice. "Riding our bikes down to the creek on a summer day. Gosh, spending the whole day just roaming around the countryside. Mr. Neely at the gas station used to give us a bottle of cola for a nickel." She sighed. "Yeah, I remember."

"Here we've got Betty at the Sunrise Café. The woman makes a homemade cinnamon roll the size of a dinner plate, I swear to you."

"The boys won't want to come home," she said quietly.

Clay waited for her to explain the odd tone in her voice. Instead, she moved on, her voice brightening a little.

"I'll call you when I have their plane reservations. You can pick them up in Billings?"

"Not a problem."

"Great, thank you, little brother. I appreciate this."

"Happy to have them. Just pack plenty of jeans and sweatshirts—toss in their hats and gloves. Do they own a winter coat?" he asked.

"Yes, they have a winter coat. They've been on a ski trip with their soccer club before."

Clay raised a brow. His nephews led far different lives than when he was a kid. "Good deal. Call me when you have things ready."

"Thanks, Clay, I'll tell the boys in the morning. They're going to be crazy happy."

That made him smile. It'd been a long time since his presence in anybody's life had made them 'crazy happy.' "Hey, Jules?" he said.

"Yeah?"

"Are you crazy happy?" He waited, the silence confirming his suspicions that not was right in her world.

"I'll call you in a couple of weeks with their flight information," she said, side-stepping his question by pulling the big sister bossy shit.

"Meantime, see if you can get a life outside of playing games online with your nephews."

Clay thought about his unorthodox agreement to help Sally Andersen. "Yeah, I'll see what I can do." After hanging up, he sat for a moment and realized how far he'd come from the brooding hermit he'd been. His stud-muffin bubble suddenly burst in his brain. How the hell was he going to manage his nephews visiting over spring break, being a part-time short order cook, and a woman who wanted him on-demand?

He'd polished his dress shoes, brushed his teeth twice, and smelled like a damn magazine insert for men's cologne. He stood at the entrance of the End of the Line high school gym feeling as though it was his first prom. Glad to finally see a familiar face coming toward him, he reached out and accepted Miss Ellie's outstretched hand.

"If I wasn't the host, young man, I'd bid on you myself." She slid her arm through his. "Come on, I'll show you to your table." She tugged him into the gymnasium.

"It looks like spring threw up in here," he commented, taking in the brightly colored décor. He'd never seen so many glittering gowns and Stetsons in one place. Two drop-down screens looped a slideshow of an historical montage of End of the Line—then and now—followed by headshots of each of tonight's bachelors participating in the auction.

"We've tried to seat you gentlemen throughout the room so you can mingle with the guests." She patted her hand on the back of a chair. The table was empty. "You're early. You'll be seated with your friend Hank. And if my memory serves, I believe, Rein and Liberty are also at this table."

"Hank, now there's a guy who should have been in this auction," Clay said with a smile. Despite his bitch of a sister, Caroline, Hank was one of his best friends. They'd lost contact after college, right after Clay joined the Army. Not everyone in his family agreed with his choice, with the exception of his grandfather back in Texas. He was a decorated WWII vet and he had no hesitancy showing his pride in Clay's enlistment. They'd written back and forth during boot camp and again when he went overseas, but his grandfather hadn't lived to see him return home. Clay had often wondered what his life might have been like had he chosen to go pro in football instead. And it always came back to the tattoo on his bicep that he'd gotten while on a leave with his buddies from camp. It'd been his grandpa's favorite saying. *These colors don't run.*

"Wow. Damn, son, you clean up fairly well."

Clay pulled from his reverie and looked across the table at Hank walking towards him. He stood and grabbed Hank's hand with a grin, then dispensing with protocol, pulled him into a bear hug. "You're as ugly as ever," Clay joked, eyeing his friend dressed in dark blue jeans, a pressed white shirt and black bolero tie. He wore a giant silver buckle on his belt, boots, and a black Stetson.

"Where the heck did you get that?" Clay pointed to the buckle.

"Montana Jewelry down in Billings. Figured I better blend in." He grinned a million-watt smile.

"It ought to be you up there, instead of me. I can see if I can arrange it," Clay offered.

Hank stopped the idea with upturned hands. "No, thank you, just the same. But I will enjoy watching you get up there." He looked around. "So where does a guy get libations around here? That was not a fun flight heading over those mountains. Radar didn't show anything, but I swear those winds seem like they're blowing something in."

Dalton walked up, a rolling cooler in tow. "Anyone here thirsty?"

Hank laughed. "Did you think this was a tailgate, bro?"

Dalton straightened his shoulders. More amazing to Clay was the Stetson Dalton wore. Angelique must have put the kibosh on his beloved Cubs baseball hat this evening. "It just so happens that I'm making a delivery to the bar. I'm supplying a few cases of my special craft beer for the occasion. I figure just because I cut out drinking doesn't mean other folks have to." He pulled out two bottles, handing one to Hank and another to Clay. "What'd you think of that first batch I sent over for you to sample?" Dalton asked him.

Clay took the frosty bottle and the opener Dalton offered next.

Dalton grinned. "What do you think of that?"

Clay studied the logo on the opener. "Kinnison Legacy?"

Dalton shrugged. "It fits."

He shrugged. "Good a name as any, I guess."

"You see the horse head? Pretty cool, right?" Dalton grinned.

There were few times Clay had seen Dalton damn near giddy about anything. The times he'd talk about the new baby on the way and building a tree house with Emilee in the backyard were just two that came to mind. This craft beer was the third.

Clay took a long pull on the bottle and licked his lips. "Yeah, I think you might be on to something here."

"Listen, I'm thinking if I can convince Dusty to go into partnership, that we could get this thing rolling right here in End of the Line. Maybe sell growlers. That's the big thing right now."

"The big thing for you right now is to get your Kinnison Legacy over to the bar."

Angelique walked up and tapped her husband's shoulder. Dressed in a long ivory gown, accented by authentic turquoise jewelry, she wore her long, dark hair loose and was the image of a beautiful statuesque mother-to-be. "Hi Clay, Hank, sorry to break up this boy's club, but my husband doesn't seem to know when to stop once he gets going on something." She smiled at him and he leaned in to kiss her.

"And you love that about me." He patted her protruding belly. "See you later."

Angelique scanned the crowd. "Have either of you seen Rein or Liberty?"

Clay shook his head. He hadn't spoken to Rein since earlier in the week to arrange his schedule. He'd been going in daily for the breakfast and lunch crowds, the café's heaviest meal times. Thankfully, she wasn't taking special occasion or large groups for the next few weeks.

Hank shrugged. "Nope, I'd think they'd be here shortly."

Clay nodded toward Wyatt and Aimee who'd just arrived. "Maybe Wyatt's heard something?"

The well-dressed pair joined them. Somber faces accompanied their attire.

"What is it?" Angelique grabbed Aimee's hand.

"Rein and Liberty can't make it. Liberty had another dizzy spell. Doc suggested that she may be dehydrated and she should get off her feet and get some fluids down her. He wants to see how she's doing in an hour or so."

Dalton appeared again without the cooler. He handed his older brother a beer. "Check out the new stock from the Kinnison Legacy. Sounds impressive, doesn't it? Hey, where's Rein and Liberty?"

Wyatt studied the bottle with a frown. "He and Liberty are staying in. She wasn't feeling well."

Dalton draped an arm around his wife's shoulder. "You think one of us should head up there and see if they need anything?"

"I suggested that when I spoke with him. He'd rather we stayed here and support Miss Ellie and Sally," Wyatt replied. "They've talked to Doc. If he needs us, he'll call." Wyatt held up the bottle. "Anyone got an opener?"

Both Clay and Hank handed him their branded Kinnison Legacy bottle openers.

Wyatt glanced at Dalton. "Bottle Openers? Next thing you'll want Dusty to sell Growlers."

"Exactly," Dalton said with a grin. "I'm seeing t-shirts, baseball caps, sweatshirts—"

"Whoa, there cowboy." Wyatt eyed Dalton. "How does this batch taste, because that stuff you sent over last week… " Wyatt made a face. "Not so great."

"Try it." Dalton urged, watching his brother carefully.

Wyatt took a swallow, considered the bottle, and nodded his approval.

"I wanted to sit down and go over some options, crunch some numbers," Dalton said.

Wyatt took another drink. "Yeah, little brother, this is good. Rein is our numbers guy. We'll talk about it at Sunday dinner."

Clay finished his beer and noticed Sally standing across the room speaking to Tyler. "If you'll excuse me, there's someone I need to talk to." He started across the room, pushing past the awkward click of his leg. With all the noise, he felt sure he was the only one that heard it, but it bothered him just the same. Before he could reach her, Sally had followed Ellie backstage and Tyler turned, walking toward him.

"Hey, look at you." Tyler slapped him on the arm, then held out his arms. "How do I look?" he asked.

"Looking good, Tyler," Clay responded, frustrated that he'd missed talking to Sally.

"Sally just told me that had record numbers of single women for the auction this year. I'm kind of hoping that Kaylee bids on me, though. I've been finding every reason on earth to stop by the clinic." He smiled. "I think she seems interested. Guess we'll see."

If Kaylee went for the shaggy, red-bearded, blue-eyed, Ed Sheeran look-a-like type, then Tyler had it going.

"It's all for Miss Ellie and the shelter, right?" Tyler said. "I could use a drink, though."

"Right, for the shelter." *And what was to become of the lusty fantasies he'd been having about Sally all week.* Clay felt a tug on his sleeve and looked down to see a set of bright blue eyes housed in a petite frame. The glasses the woman wore gave the illusion of her eyes being twice their size. She wore a powder blue gown and a lavender sweater, and if he wasn't mistaken, those were white Crocs under that gown.

"Yes, may I help you? Do you need an escort back to your seat?" He took the elderly woman's hand and patted it.

She squinted at him, her gaze taking him in from head-to-toe, lingering at times to the point of uncomfortable. She did a once-over glance at Tyler in his tuxedo.

"Just checking out the goods. I've saved all year for this. Aim to get my money's worth." She looked back at Clay, pointing a well-manicured albeit crooked finger, at him. "And I know where I'm seated young man, I may be old, but I'm not senile…not yet, anyway."

Clay watched in shock as the woman started to walk away, her pace slow and calculated. She pivoted suddenly on those sensible shoes. "And don't think I haven't got a couple of moves left in me, young man. Just been waitin' for the right one to come along."

From behind, he heard Tyler chuckling. He glanced back and found him looking at the floor, his shoulders shaking as he tried to hold in his laughter.

The spry, barely five-foot senior citizen, toddled away.

"I think she's gunning for you, Saunders." Tyler grinned. "See you backstage after dinner."

Clay stood a moment more scanning the room, hoping to spot Sally to no avail. "All for Miss Ellie," he muttered. He walked back through the now-crowded tables, artfully dodging a few jaunty finger waves by women who caught his eye.

He sat down next to Hank, nodding with a smile as his friend introduced him to the guests seated at the table. Two seats—Rein's and Liberty's—remained empty.

"How are your nephews doing?" Hank asked a few moments later as they enjoyed their steak dinner.

Clay accepted another Kinnison legacy beer from the waiter. "Things have been better since I was out there over the holiday. Here, I've got some pictures." He pulled out his cell phone to show him some of the candids they'd taken at Christmas. Julie's husband had been absent in all but one, that was Christmas morning. He handed the phone to Hank. "My nephews are almost taller than their mom. I've been playing games online with them since I came back. So things are good there. Who knew that a game system would bring me closer to my nephews, right?"

Hank nodded as he studied the pictures. "Your sister is still a knock-out." Hank glanced at Clay. "I mean that in a good way, not like a creeper way."

He looked back at the picture. "I remember going out there in our freshman year, just after your mom moved out there, I think. Julie was engaged and I remember thinking, wow, that guy is one lucky SOB." He looked up at Clay and frowned. "What was his name?"

"Louis," Clay said.

"Oh, right, does he go by Louie, or Louis?"

"Definitely Louis."

He handed the phone back. "I'm glad that things have worked out. Good lookin' family they have there."

"The guys are coming out to stay with me over spring break."

Hank smiled. "Staying with Uncle Clay." He dug into his dinner.

Clay flipped through the photos, remembering Julie's voice over the phone. Why hadn't he noticed the dark circles under her eyes in these pictures before now?

"So, you mentioned something about it being a record crowd of single women tonight?" Hank had the whole billionaire cowboy thing going on and Clay suspected that if he chose to, his friend could have his pick of several ladies in the crowd. "You have your sights on anyone in particular?"

Clay glanced toward the stage and saw Sally talking to Dusty. He was helping emcee the event with Miss Ellie. They seemed to be going through a script of sorts and Sally appeared to be patiently walking through the steps of his responsibilities. He doubted she'd had a bite to eat.

She looked up and though the stage lights were far too bright for her to see, he kept his gaze on her, taking in the silver and black gown that was modest in covering, yet fit her every curve. The look was perfection. His fingers itched trying to determine if the zipper was in back or along the side.

"Hey, isn't that Sally Andersen?" Hank nudged Clay and followed his blatant stare. "Man, she is still as pretty as ever."

"Yeah." Clay polished off his beer and reached for the glass of wine the waiter had poured for dinner.

"Whoa, there, Romeo. You want to be able to navigate those steps," Hank cautioned.

Clay heeded his advice, though the real question in Clay's mind was how he was going to navigate that dress.

CHAPTER SEVEN

Sally thought she might go crazy. She'd been putting out so many fires this evening, she would surely qualify to be a smokejumper. Taking a deep breath, she took a sip of the deep, rich red wine they'd served with her now cold steak. The salad, gratefully, was wonderful and she cleaned it up quickly before something else could grab her attention. She'd managed to get Dusty and Ellie comfortable in their roles as emcees for the auction and had decided to sneak back to her seat for a quick bite before the auction started.

"Do you need to be backstage to help line up the bachelors?" Angelique asked. She and Dalton were seated at her table, along with Nate and Charlene, and a couple from Billings.

Sally shook her head after taking another swallow of wine, letting it calm her frazzled nerves. "Nope, Miss Ellie has it covered. Dusty's got the cards for introductions." She raised her glass. "Here's hoping that everything pulls off without a hitch." Her hand raised in toast, she noticed Clay skirting around the edge of the crowd of women beginning to amble to the chairs set in front of the stage. He looked handsome, amazing to be exact, with those broad straight shoulders and trim physique. She fought the reins of her galloping heart as she remembered what lay beneath that starched white shirt.

"I hope you've saved your pennies, girlfriend."

Sally looked over her shoulder at the kind-looking elderly woman who'd stopped to speak to her.

"Why, Miss Eva, hello. I'm so glad you made it tonight. How are you?" Sally squeezed the woman's hand. "You are a vision of loveliness." She eyed the pale blue gown that nearly matched the woman's clear blue eyes. Her head tilted as she spied the white Crocs.

"Sensible shoes tonight. Can't do heels like I used to, but I still got a move or two inside me." Her smile was sweet. She gave Sally a nudge. "I remember your dad when he came in to the Center for his physical therapy. He was a good man." She nodded. "A real fine man." She patted Sally's shoulder. "But tonight…I have my sights set on one in particular."

"Oh, who's that?" Sally played along, shooting a winking glance to Angelique.

"That tall drink of handsome with shoulders like a Buick. If that isn't military stock, I'll eat my Crocs."

Angelique caught Sally's eye and smiled.

"You'd best be finding a good seat, young lady, if you plan on bidding. And seeing how you're the head honcho of this gig, it seems only fitting that you'd participate."

"She's right, you know," Angelique interjected.

Aside from the concerns about the event itself, Sally had been in a self-imposed battle all week, trying to decide if what she'd proposed to Clay was fair. What little she knew of him, and for the better, the more she realized he wasn't the type that would easily give up his rights or responsibilities if he was a father. Perhaps deep down, she was afraid if she started this affair with him, would she be able to give the relationship up as easily when it came time to do so.

She spied Kaylee taking her seat in the front row. The woman was determined, it seemed, as were the over seventy-five women signed up for the event. A cold dread washed over her. What if someone else, besides Miss Eva, had her sights on Clay? She did have a contract ready. After the sexy episode in her front room in the middle of the night she'd had some seriously hot dreams that included Clay.

And she'd set aside a small amount she'd intended to donate to the cause anyway. Sally pushed from the table.

Angelique and Dalton applauded. "Go get 'em, tiger," Angelique said with a grin. Of course, no one except Clay knew what rode on her winning him for the evening. She found an empty chair at the end of a row, in case she lost her nerve. Miss Eva was seated beside her.

Caught up in the jubilant frenzy of bidding, she cheered on as each bachelor was awarded to the highest bidder. Tyler was beaming as walked off stage, and met Kaylee, who gave him a chaste peck on the cheek.

Clay was the last to appear on stage. He heart came to a standstill as the room grew quiet. He offered a tight smile and a quick wave to the crowd of women poised at his feet, paddles at the ready.

Sally scanned the still significant group of anxious women that would compete against her.

"Now, ladies, we all know you're excited to know more about our next bachelor candidate." Dusty patted Clay's shoulders. "Welcome Clay to our annual Buckle Ball. Like the others, we'd like to ask you to tell us a bit about yourself." He handed the microphone to Clay.

Clay nodded and calmly looked out over the crowd. "I'm fairly new to End of the Line. Born and raised in Texas."

A 'yee haw!' went up from a woman in the crowd.

Clay smiled. "Other than that, I'm a pretty simple guy, I guess."

Miss Ellie stepped up beside him, feigning a swoon as she used her hand to fan her face. "Okay, one question we'd like you to answer for us. What is your idea of a perfect date?" The answers from the other bachelors had been everything from candlelit dinners and a carriage ride to white-water rafting on a Colorado river.

Sally found herself pulled forward in her seat, waiting, wanting to know more about him, even though she knew it was dangerous to her heart to do so.

Clay cleared his throat. "You know, there was a time when I thought the way to a woman's heart was to try to impress her with fancy restaurants and beautiful jewelry—"

"It doesn't hurt," a woman yelled out, and laughter followed.

Clay chuckled, and the deep rich sound of it brought gooseflesh to Sally's bare arms.

"I guess my experience has taught me that a fireplace on a snowy evening, or standing in a barn talking away a rainy afternoon can mean as much to the right woman."

"Oh, hell, yeah!" called out a female voice. "Start the bidding."

Sally straightened in her seat, suddenly torn with guilt that her monogamous edict could well destroy what possible happiness Clay might find here tonight.

"Get your paddle ready, honey," Miss Eva said.

She looked at the elderly woman. "I'm not really sure about this."

Miss Eva's blue eyes twinkled behind her thick lens. "I watched that young man all evening and you know what I saw?"

Sally shook her head.

"He was watching you," she said, pointing her paddle at Sally.

"What if I'm not the right person for him?" Sally asked, glancing at the women around her. The sound of their excited whispers caused her to have doubt.

Miss Eva looked at her with a puzzled expression. "Sweetheart, it's one night. It's not like you're going to have his baby." The old lady smacked her lightly on the head. "Besides, I know men. That one there is a keeper."

Sally felt sick.

"We'll start the bidding at one hundred dollars," Dusty's voice called out across the room.

Miss Eva's hand shot out into the air, immediately followed by three other avid bidders.

"We've got one-hundred thirty-five," Dusty announced.

"One hundred fifty," Sally found herself yelling out.

Miss Eva patted her leg and smiled.

"Two hundred," another woman bid.

"Two hundred fifty," came the next bid.

"Three hundred."

Sally's gaze shot to Nan of the sporting goods and repair store in town.

"Three-fifty," Miss Eva countered with a pursing of her lips. "That woman has another thing coming if she thinks she can outbid me."

It felt as though a cattle drive thundered in Sally's chest.

"One thousand," issued a firm, slow-speaking, female voice.

Sally searched the crowd of women and found a beautiful, statuesque woman standing with her paddle held high. She wore a skin-tight, red-sequined gown that glittered sin. Her pale blonde hair fell over her bronzed shoulders, one side swept up over one ear in a gemstone clip. Icy-looking diamonds dripped wealth from her earlobes. Sally doubted the woman owned a single pair of boots. She glanced at her plain strand of pearls.

"Oh, my." Miss Eva glanced at Sally. "You may be on your own now, sweetheart." She shrugged her boney shoulders.

Sally had no idea how high the woman was willing to bid, but she had to try—if not for underpaid grade school teachers everywhere. "One thousand-fifty." She blinked at the very words that had come from her mouth.

The distinguished woman shot her a look.

Pride. Stupidity. She wasn't really sure. Sally stood, tightening her grip on the paddle.

"That's my girl," she heard Miss Eva say quietly.

The room was deadly silent. Several women between lowered into their seats, avidly watching the spectacle.

"One thousand, one hundred." The woman kept a steady gaze on Sally.

"One thousand, one hundred-fifty," Sally answered.

"Throw down," a male voice called out from behind. She didn't have to look to know it was Dalton.

The beautiful woman appeared to mull over her next move. She glanced at Sally, then looked at Clay. "Two thousand."

"Shit." Miss Eva clamped her hand over her mouth and glanced up at Sally.

Dusty didn't bother to hide his surprise. "Let's remember that this is all going to a wonderful cause."

Clay stood quietly, looking straight ahead in a military-style at-ease pose.

"We've got two thousand." Dusty looked at Clay. "Do I hear two-thousand, one hundred?"

Sally raised her paddle.

"There's two thousand, one hundred. Do I hear two-thousand, one hundred fifty?" Dusty took out a kerchief and dabbed his brow.

The woman in red raised her paddle. "Two thousand, one hundred-fifty."

"I've got five hundred dollars, Sally" Eva said, touching Sally's elbow. "It's yours."

Sally licked her lips. She looked at Clay and back at the woman, whose back was turned.

"The bid is two thousand, one-hundred fifty," Dusty reminded the crowd.

She had only a few thousand left in her savings after paying for her renovations. She eyed the woman even as Dusty began the protocol to end the bidding.

"Going once—"

"Two thousand, five hundred," Sally interrupted. She immediately looked down at Eva who nodded in return. Applause erupted behind her.

Miss Ellie grabbed the mic from Dusty. "Going once, twice, sold—for two thousand, five hundred." She dropped the mic, and as it clattered to the stage, she hooked her arm through Clay's and escorted him backstage.

Slightly flustered, Dusty picked up the mic. "Thanks to all the winners. We'll take just a few minutes to set up the band and then we'll start the dance."

Sally was rushed by well-wishers and Miss Eva stood to hug her.

"I knew you'd win. I can see how you look at him." She winked. "But if you don't mind, since I have five hundred bucks invested, I'd like just one dance."

"Absolutely." Sally hugged the woman and turned to find Clay and Miss Ellie waiting behind her.

"The band is setting up. I better get back to my post." Ellie came forward and hugged Sally. "Thank you for your generosity. I feel you got the best tonight," she whispered then stepped back. "You two have fun."

Clay was talking to Angelique and Aimee. Sally stepped up and brazenly hooked her arm through his. "Well, I guess the first order of business is a drink, and sorry, I'm not buying." She smiled at her friends, but had yet to look at Clay.

Wyatt, Dalton and Hank joined them then after they'd helped move the chairs from the dance floor.

"Congratulations, young man." Miss Eva tapped Clay's chest with her paddle. "The best woman won."

"And Clay will save you that dance, don't forget." Sally patted Clay's arm.

"Dance?" Clay leaned downed to whisper in her ear.

She turned to look at him, meeting his dark gaze. Holy Moly. All the old fears, the guilt washed over her. She'd wanted to believe she could slide through this with the grace of a glacier, but global warming had nothing on her body heating when she was near him. To make matters worse, or better—depending on your view—she'd taken her temperature this morning as she'd been keeping a chart these past few months to track her peak ovulation. Her girl parts fairly screamed with joy as she held his gaze. *How soundproof are the rooms backstage*, flitted through her brain.

"Sally?" Clay asked, his brows knit with concern.

"Hum? Yes?"

"You're doing that 'checking-out' thing again."

"Oh, sorry. I promised Miss Eva you'd dance with her. Since she invested the last five hundred into my bid."

Clay's expression softened. "That's a lot of money, Sally." He turned his head so others couldn't hear. "Let me help you with this."

She glanced at him and, between being broke and her raging hormones, spoke the first thing on her mind. "Hopefully, you can." She held his eyes for a moment, smiled and turned back to their friends.

"You really made Miss Eva's night, you know," Sally said as she carefully removed her pearl earrings and necklace and tucked them into a blue velvet box.

"She's a sweet little lady." Clay sat in the corner of her bedroom, slouched in a floral patterned reading chair that was two sizes too small. He'd loosened his tie, was itching to get out of the starched shirt, but didn't want to appear too anxious. Truth? He was damn exhausted.

"Did anyone ask where you were going?" Sally glanced at him. He'd been engrossed in studying the three page, single-spaced contract she'd had drawn up, she'd told him, by a legal site online. No way in hell he planned on missing this chance. He stood and slipped off his jacket, stuffed the tie in the pocket and walked up behind her.

"Oh." She shot him a quick glance, her beautiful cheeks blushed crimson.

"Let me do that." He eased her hands to her sides and leaned forward to place a kiss on the corkscrew tendrils at the back of her neck. He'd thought about this more times than he cared to admit. Unfastening the clip, he threaded his fingers through her hair, fascinated in watching it tumble in rich, red waves over her bare shoulders. His fingers brushed her skin and he heard a soft gasp, felt her body stiffen. He moved closer, breathing in her scent, something floral, sexy and so like Sally. A mystery, a mustang—all woman. He wanted her out of that gown, and his hands moved over the front of her following every curve. "I've been trying to decide if the zipper is on the side or in the back." Half aroused already, he realized she wore no bra beneath all this glitter.

"The side," she purred, leaning back into him.

He spied the zipper, eased it down partway and slipped his hand inside covering her bare breast.

"Oh, okay," she said, releasing a breathy sigh. "Before we go any further, there's a couple of things we should talk about."

"Are you having second thoughts?" He rolled her rosy nub between his fingers, eliciting the languid response he'd hoped for.

"N-not exactly." She looked over her shoulder. "I need you to do something for me."

He chuckled. "I thought that's why I was here."

She turned to face him then. "I meant about the contract."

He eyed her. "I've read it, and agreed to everything, and signed it."

Sally swallowed, visibly nervous about something. "Thank you. I think it's best for both of us, don't you?"

"Sally." He leveled her a direct look, hoping to make her see she was killing the mood. "My knowledge is limited on some things, but I'm pretty certain no one has ever been conceived by lengthy discussions."

She nodded. "I know, but what I have to say… might cause you to change your mind. And I wouldn't hold it against you if you did. But I feel I need to be honest with you."

Despite the cold water moment to his libido, he appreciated her desire to be transparent. "Okay, what is it?"

"I... I can't quite pay you what I indicated in the contract—that is, unless you're willing to take payments."

"Sally," he said, softening his voice, "money is the last thing on my mind, right now."

She wrung her hands and then looked at him. "I just want you to understand. I used most of what I'd planned to give you on bidding for you."

He ran his hands down her arms. "Then let's consider it even. It's what I'd planned to do with the money, anyway. Now," he lowered his head, brushing his lips to hers with a teasing smile. "At some point, this night becomes less about talking"—he gently bit her lower lip— "and more about doing."

"I haven't done this in a while," she said breathlessly. Her hands cupped his face, her mouth demanding, seductive… in short, driving him mad with need.

"Like riding a bike," Clay whispered, brushing his mouth along her jaw. God, she smelled like heaven.

Her fingers tugged his shirt from the waistband.

"Hang on, sweetheart. This is a rental." He stepped back, his gaze holding her appreciative, smoldering gaze. He removed his shirt and tugged his undershirt over his head.

"You look like a fantasy from a James Bond movie," she said, reaching out tentatively to touch him, tracing the tattoo over his heart.

He hooked the skinny straps of her gown with his fingers, drawing it past her waist, letting it slither the rest of the way to the floor. His gaze traveled past those lips he already loved to taste and stopped. "What the hell... are those?" Clay blinked, then peered at the flesh-colored flowers covering her breasts.

"Oh," she hunched over to cover herself, grimacing as she quickly removed each one. "They're meant to lift your... breasts when you don't wear a bra with a tight gown."

Seduction, as a rule—at least for him—had never held much humor. He glanced away, covering his mouth to hide his grin.

She batted his shoulder. "Don't hurt yourself by holding it in. Go on, laugh. Guys don't have to worry about stuff like this." She frowned, absentmindedly rubbing her breasts.

Oh, hell, yeah. His dick snapped to attention. Clay eyed her as he cleared his throat. "You are...without a doubt, the most unpretentious woman I've ever met." He touched her cheek, watching her expression soften. "You don't know how beautiful you are, do you?"

She blinked and looked away, seemingly embarrassed by his tender remark. He was equally surprised. Poetic words had never come easy for Clay.

"I-I've never thought about it."

He smiled. "Your breasts are perfect, Sally." He curled his hand around the back of her head and brought her lips to his. She pulled him to the edge of the bed and savoring one more kiss, he took a step back. Old wounds from his past crept into his brain. He raked his hand though his hair, sighed, and tried a diplomatic approach. "Sally," Clay said. He took a step back, his hands on his hips. "Let's just acknowledge the elephant in the room."

She tilted her head, a smile curling her tempting lips. Her gaze lowered to where his erection tented his trousers.

He ran his hand down his face and blew out a sigh. "My leg, I'm talking about my leg."

"Your leg?" she asked, scooting to the edge of the bed. "Oh, I see. Well, is there a position that's more comfortable for you?"

He raised his brows. He hadn't expected that answer. Hell, she still had the bedside light on. Given his ex-fiancée's reaction, he assumed she'd need some time to get used to it. Or that, in fact, it might completely change her mind about being with him.

His gaze met hers. "You mean it doesn't bother you?"

Sally leaned forward and dipped her fingers over his waistband, drawing him close. She unfastened his trousers. "I don't know, maybe you better show me."

His hand covered hers, halting the task. "I'm not kidding here."

She studied him a moment, before responding. "This is about your fiancée, isn't it?"

He hated to admit it, but as long as they were being transparent. "Yes."

"You want to know what I think?" She took his hands and drew him to sit beside her. "I think she did us all a favor. If things hadn't gone as they did, you might never have come to the ranch... to End of the Line." She shrugged and gently pushed him back on the bed. "Besides, just one less appendage to tangle with," she said, unzipping his fly. "And there's only one that really matters to me right now." She smiled. "I've done my research, Clay Saunders. I figure we're only limited by our imaginations."

He sat up, capturing her face in his hands as he kissed her. It was fierce, hard. All the pain, the rejection coalesced into a powerful need to please her.

She scooted to the headboard, resting on her elbows as she watched him remove the rest of his clothes and unlatch his leg in what seemed very little time. Her eyes grew wide as he crawled toward her. He couldn't avoid what life had thrown at him. But he was lean, hard, ripped from a flawless workout regime and work on the ranch. Freed from his jockey's, his proud erection was, quite frankly, a thing of beauty.

"Forgive me." Her gaze bounced up to his. "But your ex... seriously stupid."

"You won't be needing these," he said, skimming her panties off and tossing them over his shoulder with a grin.

Having no need for protected sex offered a wild kind of indulgence. He covered her body, sliding into her tight warmth, wasting no time with soft words. Their love-making was primal. Curling her legs around him, she rose to meet his every thrust, her fingers pressing into the hard muscle of his butt as she held him close.

His body was on fire, blinded by the power he felt in the freedom of her acceptance. Clay felt an inexplicable pleasure as he watched her facial expressions, heard her soft sighs—how, lost in bliss, her lids fluttered shut.

"Sally." Clay wanted her to open her eyes, yet when she looked up at him, he was slammed with desire, yes, but also with something more than the connection they shared. "How are we doing?" he asked, hanging on by sheer willpower.

She grabbed the head board, and, arching her back, locked into his gaze with a look of challenge. He grabbed her hip, shifting his angle as he quickened his thrusts. His desire to see her pleasure drove him until, with a soft, sigh, her body closed around him. Only then, did Clay follow her over, his body trembling with the intensity of his own release.

Crazy. Amazing. Catching his breath, he braced on his elbow, their bodies still fused, and waited.

She turned her head and reached up to touch his cheek. A sheen—*were those tears*—caused her eyes to glisten. "I don't think the leg will be an issue."

He leaned down and touched his lips softly to hers. Damn. That was a mistake. Too close. Too intimate. He searched her eyes, hoping for something profound to enter his mind. "Did I see a bathroom upstairs? Did you need to...?"

"Oh, no, I'm good. It's just outside the door on the left." Clay drew on his briefs and maneuvered his leg in place. He thought about what he was doing. Sally had turned out to be more than he'd planned. She wanted sex. For a specific purpose, yes, but not with intimacy. He'd thought that after all he'd been through, all that had happened, that wall he'd built around his heart was a perfect candidate for this particular mission. But something had shifted, causing that perfect wall to crack. And he cautioned himself that he couldn't allow himself to be hurt by a woman again. He walked back into the bedroom, and just when he thought his armor was intact, she threw him a curveball.

"What in God's name are you doing?" He walked around the end of the bed and sat down next to her. She had her long legs propped vertically on the headboard, the sheets drawn over her to cover her nakedness. Her ankles were crossed and he noted the splashes of her hot pink toenail polish.

"Giving your swimmers every possible chance to hook up down there," she answered, glancing up at him. "I read it in a medical journal that it can help."

He wondered if he might ever tire of how she could surprise him. He chuckled and shook his head.

"I like it when you laugh. Even if it is at my expense." She smiled.

This was borderline dangerous. First great sex, then laughter, and pretty soon she'd be making him coffee some morning. "I have to say, I've never met anyone quite like you, Sally Andersen." He lay back on the bed, for the first time in a great while—content.

"May I ask you something? And please," she said, turning her head to look at him, "tell me, if it's none of my business."

He propped up on his elbows. "Okay, I'm listening."

"Did you know that woman tonight?" she asked, plucking a thread on the sheet.

"There were a lot of women there tonight, Sally. Which one?"

She glanced at him. "The gorgeous woman in the red dress who looked like she'd stepped out of Vogue magazine."

"Oh, you mean Dr. Lawrence?" He'd seen her arrive, offered a pleasant hello, but hadn't lingered, hadn't a desire to linger. She reminded him of his ex. All make-up and glitter. Little substance, aside from her book smarts.

"So you did know her?"

He nodded. "I do. She happens to be the clinical psychologist that I went down to Billings to see for a time."

Sally shot him a shocked look.

"Sally, I can almost hear your brain going from zero to sixty about now. And yes, we did have dinner a couple of times, after she released me with a clean bill of mental health. Was there something huge between us? No. It was sex, a lot like—" He stopped.

"You can say it. Just like us," she said, averting her gaze.

"Sally," Clay started.

Sally chuckled. "Yeah, let's talk about the elephant in the room." She pressed her lips together. "You probably ought to go. It's getting late. We don't need this to get all over town."

She stared at the ceiling as he dressed and he started to leave, wondering if the next time they met on the street, it would be awkward. There wasn't even a 'call you later' or 'until next time'. It left him unsettled.

It wasn't the kind of news you wanted to hear while flipping pancakes on a Tuesday morning. He'd come in to help with the morning crowd, due to Betty's Tuesday specials designed for the many delivery trucks with scheduled stops in End of the Line. The counter was full, as were most of the tables. There'd been no slowdown of breakfast platters since they opened at six a.m. Still, in the kitchen where he and Angelique were busy, the silence was deafening. It was as though a vacuum had sucked the joy out of the day.

"I should have gone out there. I should have insisted she go to Billings right away."

Clay stepped around the counter and put one arm around her. "There's nothing more anyone could have done, Angelique. It's not fair. But sometimes nature knows best. We're lucky that Liberty is okay. Losing a baby is terrible for both of them, but if Rein had lost them both…." He shook his head.

"I know. I just feel so bad for her. She wanted that baby so much."

"Another short stack with two sunshines and bacon," Betty said as she carried some empty plates to the sink. Her eyes were red, swollen. "Aw, sweetheart. Why don't you go on home? You've been here since dawn. Go on and tend to your family. They need you right now."

Angelique left and after lunch the crowd finally dwindled. Clay was about to take a break. He hadn't seen or heard from Sally since Saturday night. He also hadn't slept a great deal between thoughts of her and the terrible news from Rein and Liberty. He looked up when he heard the back door open. There stood Sally, without a coat, her keys dangling in her hand. Her expression was grief-stricken. She'd been crying.

"You heard?"

He nodded and held out his arms.

She didn't hesitate, but ran to him, burying her face in his shirt. Her hot tears soaked through his T-shirt.

News that Liberty had lost the baby spread quickly through town. He expected Sally wouldn't take the news well.

She sniffed and stepped back, wiping her eyes. "I feel so selfish, Clay. And scared, and selfish that I feel scared, because I'm thinking more about me and I should be thinking about Liberty and… poor Rein." Her sad, red-rimmed eyes looked up at him. She opened her mouth to speak, but shook her head.

Clay took her by the shoulders. He couldn't at this moment go into how it made him feel that she'd sought him in her time of need. He wondered if she even realized it herself. "Sally, this doesn't mean it's going to happen to you, or to Angelique." He tipped her chin to meet his gaze. "Or that you have any less of a right to want to have a baby of your own."

Her chin wobbled and she stepped into his embrace. God, the wall around his heart was crumbling by the moment. A sobering thought settled in his brain and it might refute some small print clause in their contract, but he needed to tell her. He held her close, resting his chin on the top of her head. "If anything like that were to happen, Sally. I'd be there for you. I want you to know that."

Her tears subsided and she leaned back to look at him.

"I mean that," he said, searching her sweet, tear-blotched face.

She took his face in her hands and drew his head to hers in a soft, lingering kiss. "I know you do."

The taste of her warm lips fanned a need inside him. He reached back, holding her head to his as he captured her mouth again. This had nothing to do with her mission and everything to do with how he'd not been able to get her out of his mind these past few days. Maybe on some deeper level, he was afraid of losing something so precious and fragile—something he never thought he'd find again in his lifetime.

"Going on a break," he called to Betty as he gently steered Sally toward the tiny employee bathroom in the corner. It was bright, decorated in typical down-home fashion. A cross-stitch, framed in a large embroidery hoop, hung on the wall, touting this was the first day of the rest of your life. A small cabinet, sink and old wooden bench holding a mason jar of fake spring flowers welcomed those who rarely used the room in comparison to the public facility.

It smelled of disinfectant and lavender, and Clay had never been so turned on as when he bolted the door and turned in time to see Sally half undressed.

"This is probably against health code," she said against his lips as she worked on his jeans.

He dragged his shirt over his head. "I'll take care of it." He lifted her to the counter, unfastened her bra, about to burst as he watched her breasts bobble free. He couldn't get enough of her mouth, coming back for more, his desire heating to her reaction of his rough caresses. She held his head as he sampled her sweet flesh, her sighs punctuated as he gently tugged her taut nipple between his teeth.

"Should we be doing this?" Sally asked in a breathless whisper.

She wore a cute plaid skirt, tights, and boots. The oval mirror behind her wobbled as he removed the latter in the blink of an eye, and she spread her legs. Sliding his hands over her thighs, she shifted closer to the edge and he moved his thumb back and forth over her clit, bringing a groan from her lips. He was about to burst. "Still wonder if we should be doing this?" he grinned against her lips.

She curled her hand in his hair. "Oh, no, this is going to happen," she said in a breathless whisper. She hopped off her perch and reached for his waistband. He finished, eyeing her as he shoved his jeans to his knees. Need consumed him, it was more than lust driving him to bend her over and enter her, relishing in her warmth. He swallowed hard from the sheer ecstasy of their joining. Maybe it was ego. Maybe pride. Maybe it was to satisfy the loneliness he hadn't realized was inside him. It wasn't pretty, least of all romantic. It was raw, powerful, I-need-to-have-you-now type sex. The most amazing, erotic sex he'd ever had. In the tiny bathroom of a small town restaurant. Who knew?

A knock sounded on the door. Sally's eyes met his in the reflection of the mirror. Both scrambled to find their clothes and get dressed.

Clay found it strange that he was as aroused watching Sally put on her clothes, as much as seeing her without them. "Uh... be out shortly," he told whomever was on the other side.

"No hurry," it was Tyler who responded. "The other restroom was occupied. Betty said I could use this one. I can wait."

Sally's eyes grew wide. "He can't find me here," she mouthed silently.

Clay shook his head. This would require recon. "Ty, man, you still out there?"

"Yeah, need more toilet paper? It's right here."

"Uh, nope. A plunger. This one broke. Can you ask Betty if she has a spare?"

Sally covered a grin.

"Oh, man. I've got one in the truck. Be right back."

Clay unlatched the door, peeked into the room, and found it empty. He waved Sally toward the back door and grabbed an apron to throw on over his jeans.

She stopped at the door, looked at him, and smiled.

The door pushed open and a surprised Tyler, plunger raised in warrior mode, looked at Sally.

"Oh, sorry, didn't see you there." He glanced at Clay. "You want me to take care of it?"

"Tell Betty thanks for the take-out," Sally tossed out.

"What take-out?" Tyler frowned at her empty arms.

Clay opened the fridge, handed Sally a plastic container of prepped salad and plucked the plunger from Tyler's hand. "I'll handle this, man. Deadly. If you catch my drift." Clay caught Sally's eyes when Tyler's back was turned and gave her a wink.

She ducked out, hiding a grin, but he prided himself that the glow in her cheeks was his doing.

As he disinfected the bathroom from the walls down, more to ease his conscience than anything, it occurred to him that he was in trouble. Serious trouble. He was falling for Sally Andersen and not just a little—the kind that had him thinking about someone to come home to every night.

Damn.

CHAPTER EIGHT

She hadn't seen him since the hot encounter they'd shared in the tiny bathroom. It had happened so fast, obviously unplanned and she'd given no time or thought to the fact that she likely wasn't ovulating—though it didn't seem to be a topic either was interested in. Driving home from school that night, she'd just received the news from Aimee about Liberty and Rein. Her heart was breaking for them when she pulled up to the stop sign, looked across and saw his truck parked in the alley behind Betty's. She'd reacted, needing to be near him, wanting to feel his arms protective around her. That had been her fantasy when she pulled in beside him. Neither had expected the hot fire that ignited between them, far exceeding any fantasy she'd ever had about any man—ever.

Now, nearly two weeks later, she sat at that same stop sign. The spot where he usually parked was empty. It was a little after four. The café would be quiet. She could use some of that. She pulled up in front and her heart—torn in many directions—took comfort in the familiar bell that tinkled above her head.

"Well, Sally, how good to see you, honey." Betty appeared from the kitchen. "Goodness, you look like you could use a cup of my chamomile tea and maybe a slice of peach pie. Rebecca brought it in fresh this morning."

"Just the tea, thanks, Betty. I'm not very hungry."

Betty brought her a cup with its own pot. She carried an extra cup of coffee on the tray.

"May I join you for a moment? The new girl I hired while Clay has been spending time with his nephews is working out beautifully."

Sally took a sip of her tea and closed her eyes to the soothing honey sweetness Betty had added on her own. "This hits the spot, thanks, Betty. How's Jerry doing?"

Betty pressed her palms to the table and let out a small sigh. "I can't believe it's almost been a month since his stroke. Fortunately, doctors don't feel there will be any permanent damage. He's regaining his strength and it had a mild effect on his speech, but that's also improving."

"That's wonderful news. It could have been so much worse."

Betty nodded and looked out the window. She dabbed her eyes with a napkin. "It would have been if not for Clay's quick thinking and how fast the EMT's got to Jerry to the Billings Clinic. Doctors said he was lucky. His stroke was caused by a clot, and they managed to use tPA within the time needed for it to be effective."

"Tissue Plasminogen Activator," Sally interjected. "I did some research on it as dad's health declined."

"That's what they called it, yes. I call it a miracle." Betty fisted her hands in front of her. "Jerry had angels surrounding him that night for certain. I'm so grateful… we both are."

"How's his rehab going?"

Betty chuckled. "I'm sure they are ready to get rid of him. He's an ornery old coot. He keeps the staff and nurses in stitches, so they tell me. He may have to use a cane for balance, at least for a time. But they say he should be able to be back to work by summer."

Sally teared up and reached out to squeeze Betty's hand. "Jerry had a lot of prayers going up for him, and for you, too, Betty."

She nodded. "That's true. You know some folks might enjoy being able to blend into the woodwork, to enjoy their anonymity, but I don't know. I feel maybe they miss out on the benefit of a close-knit community."

Sally thought of the numerous times she'd despised End of the Line for that very reason—choosing to see it from the life-in-a-fishbowl status, rather than as 'close-knit.'

"And you, baby doll? How are you?" Betty patted Sally's hand. "How did your evening with Clay Saunders go? I haven't had the chance to ask. He certainly seems to be adjusting well to our little town."

Sally took another sip, stalling with her answer. Her stomach suddenly felt queasy. She hated to think what some of her 'close-knit' neighbors would think of her clandestine affair with Clay for the express purpose of having a child. "It was a pleasant evening." Sally smiled. "And we raised a lot of money for Miss Ellie, which was the best part of the evening." She chose to set aside her personal opinion on what was *really* the best part of the evening for her. "You know, maybe I will take a piece of that pie to go. Oh, and maybe some soup? What do you have on today?"

"Your favorite," Betty beamed. "Potato Wild Rice." She stood, wiping her hands on her apron. "I need to get ready for the supper crowd, anyway. Let me box that up for you."

Sally gathered her coat and purse, turning when she heard the bell over the door and saw Rein and Liberty walk inside. She'd spoken a couple of times on the phone to Liberty, but hadn't seen her since the sad news. Liberty caught Sally's gaze and walked over. The two shared a warm embrace, and Sally held her friend tight. No words were spoken. None were needed. She saw Rein standing near and reached for him, pulling him close.

"It's going to be okay, Sal. It's going to be okay," he whispered as he hugged her.

"It's so good to see you guys," she said, moving aside so they could sit down.

"I was ready to get out of the house a little bit." Liberty smiled, touching Rein's arm. "Everyone is meeting here for supper. I needed a change of scenery."

"Why don't you join us?" Rein suggested, helping his wife out of her coat.

Sally loved the thoughtful gesture which, in her opinion, set apart the Kinnsion men in comparison to many others these days. She shook her head. "May I take a raincheck? I've got a night of entering grades ahead of me. They have to be in before Friday."

Rein nodded and checked his watch. "We decided to come in early before it gets too crowded."

Sally grinned. "Welcome to my world. Teachers and senior citizen's hour. Best time to get a seat."

"Is Clay joining us?" Liberty asked with a not-so-subtle glance at Sally.

"He was going to try. He took his nephews back to the airport today. Their flight was four-thirty, I think." He turned to Sally. "Did you meet those two? Good kids. They love their uncle, that's for sure."

She shrugged. "No, I'm afraid I didn't get the chance." She felt an odd disconnect that Clay had spent the last week with his nephews, but she hadn't met them. School in End of the Line, however, was still in session. Even so, there was no real reason she should expect him to make the effort to introduce them to her. They weren't exactly dating. Not even really close friends. It was kind of depressing in truth. "Hey, you all have a wonderful supper. See you soon." She waved goodbye, picked up her supper, and as she pulled from the parking spot, noticed Clay's truck turning the corner in her rearview mirror.

She sighed. Maybe it was best that their lives seemed on opposite paths, their lives intersecting only in brief moments of monumental sexual bliss. Yeah, hard to put *that* too far on the back burner.

Two days later, Sally sat in front of her laptop at her kitchen island. Stacks of papers surrounded her. She removed the reading glasses she sometimes used when working on the computer for extended periods of time. She glanced at her tea cup, then the microwave clock, taken aback when she noticed it was past eleven o'clock. Pushing her hair back, she stretched her arms overhead, working a kink out of her lower back. She hadn't eaten, forgotten actually while focusing on getting her grades entered before the Easter break.

She walked over and placed her cup in the microwave, then punched in sixty seconds. Fifty. Forty. Thirty. Sally blinked at the realization that one minute had passed from her life. Gone forever. She stared at the numbers, seeing the stark reality of her life equated in a digital countdown.

An insistent sound pulled her from her reverie. There was a knock on her back door. Curious, she stood on tiptoe to look through the peephole and then opened the door.

Clay stood there looking at her. Fresh snowflakes glittered in his dark hair.

"Is that fried chicken I smell?" She nodded toward the bag in his hand.

"Probably my coat. It was hanging in the back while I was cooking." He held up the bag. "Late night snack?"

She took the bag. "I haven't eaten. Come on in."

"Are you feeling okay? Betty mentioned the other night that you didn't feel well."

She placed the bag on the counter. Her tea had finished and she took it out. Suddenly the food didn't hold the same appeal as when he was holding it.

"Clay."

"Sally," they said in unison, then laughed.

"Did you stop by just to bring me chicken?" she asked, wrapping her hands around the warm mug to stabilize her nerves.

"I don't want to lie to you," he said.

"Then don't."

"And I don't want to frighten you if you're not ready to hear what I have to say."

She tightened her grip, bracing for the inevitable. He wanted out of the contract. It was clear that spending time with his nephews had made him realize what he had. He was going to go back to California.

"I love you."

The mug slipped from her grasp, shattering to the floor.

"Jesus," he said with a sigh. "That's how I thought you might react. Sorry about the cup." He bent down to pick up the bigger shards at her feet as her brain puttered to jump start from its immediate shutdown.

She tapped his shoulder.

He glanced at her, stood, and tossed the broken pieces in the trash. He washed his hands.

"Did you say—?"

"I love you? Yes, Sally, I did." He wiped his hands on a dishtowel.

She hadn't moved. Couldn't, actually. Her tongue seemed glued to the roof of her mouth. Even more when he scooped her into his arms and carried her to the back door.

"You need to get a broom to pick up the small pieces. Be careful going barefoot in there until you do." He started to leave.

What the hell? "Wait a second," she said, finally finding her voice as she grabbed his coat sleeve. "You come in here and drop that bomb, then don't even give me a chance to say how I feel about all this?"

He eyed her, then looked away, before speaking. "I don't expect a response, Sally. I just felt I needed to tell you. I wasn't sure how'd you feel about continuing with your plan." He blew out a weary sigh. "I thought maybe you'd need to find someone… more detached." He shook his head. "I don't know what I thought. But I've been thinking a lot about this and, well, that's what I concluded. I love you, plain and simple. You may think I'm crazy." He raised a brow and shrugged. "Pretty certain you wouldn't be the first."

"And in all this consideration you've done, did it ever occur to you what it was I needed?"

"I only know what you've told me, Sally, and that is you want a baby."

"I do, if its meant to be, but I want you, Clay."

He shrugged again. "In my defense, you could do a hell of a lot worse than me… wait—what?"

"I said, shut up and kiss me." She framed his face. Those exquisitely beautiful green eyes held hers.

"I want to be clear, Sally." He paused, searching her eyes. "I need to know this… whatever it is, is more than just sex. He tossed her an impish grin. "Don't get me wrong. Sex with you has been off the charts. But I want more. I always have. I wasn't looking for this…you. But, I know I've never felt—"

"I love you, too," she interrupted.

That silenced him. She smiled and kissed him softly. "I love you."

He picked her up and held her tight against his chest. She hugged his neck.

She showered him with kisses as he tried to navigate down the narrow corridor to the stairway. She sat on the steps watching as he carefully hung up his coat and then leaned over, brushing his mouth to hers. His hand inched beneath her camisole, slowly stripping away her inhibitions, replaced by a familiar raw hunger that he brought out in her. Holding her close, he slipped his hand between her thighs, drawing her to another high, floating on pure sensory overload. She lay back on the stairs, her clothes askew, wanting him— surrendering her body to whatever the future with him entailed.

"Race you upstairs," he said, grinning against her mouth

Sally didn't think sex could get much better with Clay, until she realized they were making love. He wanted to be there, wanted her as much as she wanted him. Having a child with him had taken on an entirely different meaning. They hadn't used contraception. Hadn't talked about it.

"Clay?" Sally lay curled beneath him, cradled beneath his arm. She traced her finger over the heart-shaped flag and dog tag tattoo over his heart.

"Yeah," he replied sleepily, his eyes shut.

"About having a child."

He opened one eye and looked at her. "I still want kids, don't you?"

Surprised by his sudden response, she smiled. "Yes, of course. I want your kids."

"Our kids." He shifted to face her, brushing her hair over her shoulder, before he leaned down to kiss the warm flesh.

"Our kids," Sally repeated. She marveled how life could change so fast. It was like something Michael was always saying, *"Sometimes you just have to grip the reins tight and hang on for the ride."* She touched the tattoo. "What do all the dog tags represent?"

He glanced down, took her hand and kissed it before placing it once more over his heart. "There's one for every member of my team that day. I was riding on top of the armored vehicle. We were checking for civilians in a bombed city. None of us saw the rocket grenade until it was too late. I was blown off in the blast. The teams behind us were able to fall back. The truck carrying the launcher took off. We responded, but there were a lot of wounded soldiers needing attention."

Sally searched his face, seeing in his eyes the moment relived. "How awful, Clay. I'm sorry seems too trite of a word."

He blinked as though pulling himself back to the present. He looked directly at her. "Aside from doctors, I've never told anyone what happened that day."

She wrapped her arms around him, wanting nothing more than to be close, to let him take comfort in her embrace, to know that it mattered to her what he'd been through, even though she'd never fully understand.

Sweat poured down his face. Desert heat consumed him. Dust filled his lungs. He swiped the

grit from his eyes, hoping to stave off the incessant stinging from the sweat droplets trickling into his eyes. Keep your eyes moving. He searched the low clay walls, pockmarked by mortar rounds. The village appeared deserted, but you never knew what might be hiding behind the blown-out building that once housed a family. A movement caught his eye. He called to the driver, leaning forward to point out the small boy darting down a narrow path. He held his hand up to caution the team behind when a flash blinded him. He felt himself propelled off the vehicle, saw the cloudless blue sky whiz past him. There was no feeling. No pain. His body slammed against the hard, clay ground like a rag doll tossed away by an angry child. All around him were small fires. His team, four men and a woman, lay motionless, many no longer recognizable, mangled pieces scattered across the sand. He looked down and in a haze saw another soldier working frantically on him, trying to tie off what was left of his leg. He had no right to live. No right.

Clay heard the sound of his own screams as he woke from the nightmare. It was dark, he couldn't see. He felt the someone's hands, shaking him and he lashed out to push them away.

"Clay, wake up! Wake up! It's Sally. You're safe, Clay. You're safe at home."

A soft light switched on. He blinked, his brain slowly realizing where he was. His body ached. His muscles were tense. He rubbed the heels of hands over his eyes, hoping to dissipate the images floating in his brain.

"Here." Sally, dressed in a pale pink bathrobe with cartoon kittens all over it, handed him a glass of water and a hand towel.

"Jesus, Sally, I'm sorry." He pushed upright, the sheets pooled around his hips, and surveyed the tangle of sheets. "Did I do that?" He looked at her, fear gripping his chest, realizing how much he must have thrashed around. "Did I hurt you?"

She sat on the bed, her legs curled under her. She shook her head. "I'm fine. I'm more concerned about you."

He closed his eyes and breathed deeply, willing his heart back to a normal pace. "I'm good." He sighed. "I'm good." He glanced at her. "I haven't had one of those in a while."

"A nightmare?"

He nodded.

"You seemed to be trying to tell someone something. I couldn't tell what you were saying."

Clay knew. And it didn't matter now.

"I'm sorry, Clay, for all you've been through, for all that you've sacrificed."

His gaze snapped to hers. "Yeah, I'm the lucky bastard who got to come home, Sally."

She pressed her lips and said nothing. Just squeezed his hand.

"I'm sorry, this isn't your fault."

"I know. Maybe there is a reason you were spared."

"Yeah, maybe. I keep telling myself that. But I haven't figured out a good enough reason yet." His throat parched, he drank the water in one long swallow, then ran the towel over his head and neck. "I'm sorry you had to experience that." He glanced around, realizing it was getting lighter outside. "What time is it?"

Sally smiled softly. "I'm not sorry, Clay. I want to be there for you when things get hard. You've been there for me more times than I can count." She reached over and slanted the blinds so that the sun's early rays peeked through. "It's past seven on a beautiful Saturday morning. And by now, everyone who has driven by has seen your truck parked on the street and has put two and two together. So, today," she said, crawling over to kiss him lightly, "I'm making you breakfast. How's that for defying the rumor mill?"

The view from his vantage point had him thinking to hell with the rumor mill. He tugged her close, kissing that lovely mouth as he loosened the robe tie. The nightmares of his past might surface now and again, but having the sanctuary of Sally's arms, her honesty and compassion, brought him a peace he'd never known. He pressed his hand against her cheek. "Maybe you should let me cook," he murmured, searching those entrancing eyes. Her robe slipped off one shoulder as she pushed him back on the bed and straddled him. "We'll see who can get downstairs faster when we're through."

He raised a brow and turned her beneath him. "Challenge accepted."

Clay hadn't been able to stop grinning for three days straight. Michael just shook his head when Clay would occasionally break into a whistle while doing chores. He and Rein had gone back to work on the remodel project in his basement. Life was good. Their relationship—what it had been elevated to—was no longer a secret in town. And the Kinnison clan couldn't have been any happier.

He drew his pencil from behind his ear to mark the spot where he'd measured twice for the island countertop that Liberty had requested for the downstairs.

"I want everyone to be able to gather here," she had told him and Rein before she went to meet Angelique. The two were going shopping for Angelique's and Dalton's baby, due in early summer.

Clay had seen all types of courage in his day, but Liberty's selfless gesture to help her sister-in-law ranked right up there with the best. "She is one strong woman," Clay told Rein after she'd left.

Rein glanced at him and nodded. "She's been through a lot. Guess maybe she's seems strong because of it. It hasn't been easy on either of us, but she's been a rock for me throughout this whole ordeal." He offered a dim smile to Clay. "I'll be glad when we can try again. Doc says give it a couple of months." Rein sighed. "I just want to be able to give her everything she deserves. The woman is selfless, loving, and she'll make a great mom. You should see how her face lights up around Gracie."

For the first time Clay understood what Rein was talking about. Though they hadn't yet had the chance to talk much about the future, he felt sure and strong about what he and Sally felt for each other.

His cell phone buzzed in his pocket and, digging it out, he saw it was Julie's number. "Stepping outside to take this," he said to Rein. "Hey Jules, what's up?" It had only been a few days since he'd sent the boys back home. "Did one of the boys leave something here? I tried to make sure all their game gear was gathered up."

"No, Clay," her voice sounded grim. "I need your help." He heard a sniff.

"Jules, are you okay? Are the boys okay?" He stood searching the tree line that separated Rein's backyard from the foothills. His instinct prickled.

"It's Louis," she said quietly, almost too calm. "I thought if we had some time alone that we could work things out."

A cold dread formed in Clay's gut. He took a deep breath, needing to ask the unthinkable. "Jules, has he hurt you or the boys?"

"Never the boys."

Shit. "That bastard. Jules, you've got to get out of there. The guy needs help. This isn't normal."

"I used to think it was the stress of his work. That eventually as he achieved his goals it would get better, but it seems to have only gotten worse." There was a pause. "I know I should leave him, Clay. Part of me wants to, but the other part is terrified. I don't know what to do, where to go."

The answer seemed clear. "Jules, I'm going to fly out and help you. Where is Louis now? Is he home?"

"N-no. He's away on business. I don't expect him home until Friday."

"Okay, honey, here's what you do. You call and reserve a truck. I'll pick it up when I get in. You get your things together. Have the boys help."

"They don't know anything about this, Clay."

He thought for a moment how astute his nephews seemed. "Chances are they know things aren't good, Jules. You need to be straight with them and ask for their help. They can handle it."

"Where will we go? We sold the farm in Texas when mom moved. Granddad is gone now."

"You'll come here and stay at the ranch until we figure things out."

"That's kind of you, Clay, but I doubt the Kinnisons had this in mind when they built this place, much less that I could afford it."

"It's exactly why they built it, Jules. Trust me. I'll take care of things on my end. You get things pulled together on yours. If he comes back, if he tries to stop you, call the police. You understand?"

There was another pause.

"Jules?"

"Yes, I understand," she said.

"I know this can't be easy, but how long have you been dealing with this?"

"Longer than I should have."

"That's what I thought. I wish you'd come to me sooner."

"You had your own issues to contend with, Clay. You didn't need some whiny sister adding to your troubles while you were trying to get your life back."

Clay shook his head. Had he been that self-absorbed? "Jules, you and the boys are all the family I have left. You are my life."

Another sniff signaled she was crying.

"Listen, you need to pull it together right now— for you, for the kids. Understand?"

"Y-yes."

"Good. Call if you need anything. I'll see you soon."

"Thank you, Clay."

"Love you, Jules. Be careful."

Clay took a deep breath, forcing himself to not imagine wringing the life out of Louis with both hands. He stormed inside. "Rein, that was my sister. Problems at home. She needs my help. Long story short—I'd like to bring her and the boys back to the ranch until we figure out what's best."

Rein frowned. "Not a problem, I'll talk to Wyatt. Is there something you need me to do?"

Clay shook his head. "I'm going to go out there and drive them back. It should only take a couple of days."

Rein nodded. "Okay, I'll go down and make sure the two-bedroom cabin is ready for them."

"Thanks, man." Rein stepped forward and gave his friend a brief hug. "As long as I know she and the boys are safe out here, I'm good."

"Is Louis home?" Rein asked.

Clay set to gathering his tools. "Out of town on business until Friday. So, she's got a good window. She'll have to pull the boys from school, of course." He hesitated at the thought.

"Talk to Sally. She might be able to get them enrolled if necessary to finish out the school year, anyway."

"Good idea, thanks." He drove straight to the little two-story clapboard with the wraparound porch. As he pulled in the gravel drive, he noted the lights glowing warm in the dusky hue of the evening. He saw Sally moving around the kitchen and the rest of that wall around his heart crumbled to ash. He'd lay down his life for her. "You are one lucky bastard," he said as he turned off the ignition.

Clay showered as Sally finished the biscuits she'd made to go with the crock-pot stew.

"Stolen from Betty," she admitted, stirring the pot and releasing an amazing aroma. "She said even I couldn't mess this up."

They sat at the kitchen island and ate as he explained the situation with his sister.

"Of course, you need to be there for her. I understand completely. How long do you think it should take?"

Clay shrugged. "It's roughly a couple of days' drive, I suspect. I'm driving a small moving truck. She and the kids can drive the rental, if she's not comfortable taking the other car. Louis liked to keep things tight. Both cars are registered in his name. The less we have to deal with him, the better."

"Miss Ellie might be able to offer her some legal advice," Sally offered. "Why don't you use my laptop and book your flight while I clean this up."

Clay checked every airline out of Billings. There was nothing available until tomorrow afternoon. He dialed Julie to check on her.

"Hello?" The pensive sound in her voice twisted Clay's heart.

"Jules. There aren't any flights until tomorrow afternoon. But I'm going to head down to the airport in the morning and see if I can get on stand-by. You doing okay?"

She sighed. "I think so. This is such a nightmare. I'm sorry to drag you into it."

"Ok, I don't want to hear you say that again." That part of Julie that once pitied him was one of his anger triggers. He took a deep breath, refocusing his thoughts. "How are the boys?"

"I told them. They didn't seem all that surprised." She chuckled softly. "I don't think I gave them enough credit for noticing things. They always seem to be glued to their video games."

"Different ways of dealing, Jules," Clay responded.

"I suppose. They did, however, seem more than okay with the idea of going back to visit their uncle."

"I wouldn't have said this a year ago, but life here in this little town is good." He looked up and caught Sally's smile from across the room. "Really good. I'll let you know when I get a flight."

"Thanks, Clay."

"Jules, I haven't done anything yet."

"You've been there. You've been a great uncle, a great brother… thank you, for everything."

"That's why I'm here. See you soon."

Later that night as Sally slept peacefully curled in close to him, he thought about what she'd said about being spared from death for a reason. As the sun peeked over the rim of the mountains, Clay kissed Sally as she slept, left her a note by the coffee pot, and headed to Billings.

CHAPTER NINE

"Arrived. Will call you later. Love you." Sally read the words on her phone as she climbed in her truck after school. The timestamp indicated they'd been sent more than an hour ago. She'd gone down to the ranch, needing to be near the horses and had taken a few minutes to speak to Michael.

Spring was on the horizon, though the threat of snow was still a reality until late April, longer in the higher elevations. But the budding of the Serviceberry trees was a sure sign of the seasons change.

She glanced up and sitting perched in front of her on a fence post was a Great White Owl. Not unusual in the region—the Crow lore believed it was a sign of an impending storm. To the Kinnison's, the owl's presence prior to a variety of unusual happenings had become a lore of their own—believing it to be the spirit of Jed Kinnison keeping an eye on his family. She'd heard their stories, even pondered the possibility of its truth, but had never seen the owl herself.

His bright yellow-gold eyes blinked at her, his gaze unwavering, almost as though he was assessing her. A strange chill washed over her as she started the truck. The owl didn't flinch. *An impending storm?*

Sally glanced at the cloudless sky in the late afternoon, then at her watch. She had enough time to go home and change before meeting for their first girl's night since Liberty lost the baby. Little Elaina Marie Mackenzie had been laid to rest in a private ceremony a few weeks before in the End of the Line cemetery next to her Grandpa Jed Kinnison.

Putting the truck into gear, she noted the owl had flown off and, for some reason, Sally released a sigh of relief. Arriving home, she dropped her book bag by the back door and went upstairs to change. She smiled when she walked into the room and noticed one of Clay's shirts folded neatly over the back of her reading chair. She picked it up and held it to her chest, breathing in his familiar scent. She marveled at how naturally the transition had taken place between them, though she had to give credit to Clay for taking them from their odd partnership to a budding relationship. She considered how, in many ways, she knew little about him, yet in other ways, she felt she'd known him a lifetime. She considered calling him, but decided that he was likely busy helping Julie and would call when he got the chance.

Thirty minutes later she sat in a booth at the cafe enjoying some new appetizer recipes that Betty had been experimenting with.

"So, Rein mentioned that Clay had to go to California to help his sister?" Liberty asked, sifting through a plate of Irish nachos made with waffle fries instead of tortilla chips.

Sally shook her head in response. "I don't understand what possesses a man to think they can hit a woman or a child and justify it. It makes no sense."

Angelique offered a sad smile. "It is a warped and very disturbed mentality. Thankfully, Miss Ellie was there to help me get out of that toxic relationship. Sometimes, you can't see the danger. You just hope that if you're good enough, things will change." Angelique sighed. "It took me almost losing my daughter to make me realize the problem wasn't me." She looked at Sally with the eyes of wisdom. "Has she been dealing with this for very long?"

"Clay didn't say. But I'd guess long enough. Thankfully, he hasn't hurt either of the boys."

"Well, Clay is doing the right thing by going out there to help her," Aimee said. "And Wyatt mentioned that he's driving them back here to stay at the ranch until she decides what to do."

Sally nodded. "Clay wants to be able to keep an eye on her and the kids. I'm going to see about getting them enrolled in school, at least for the remainder of the semester. Then we'll see what happens."

"Okay, girls, try these." Betty set a plate down in front of the four women. "These are little puff pastries I've been working on. I've got some with a Boston cream filling and some with a buttercream filling. Tell me which you think is best."

"Anything for a good cause, Betty." Angelique popped one in her mouth and licked her fingertips. She rolled her eyes heavenward. "Those are amazing."

"Oh, good. Would you all mind tasting my lemon bars?"

"Maybe we should order supper before we eat more sweet stuff," Sally suggested.

"Killjoy." Angelique made a face and smiled as she tossed another pastry in her mouth. She chewed the sweet concoction and looked at Betty. "So, what's with all the new recipes, Betty? Not that I mind, clearly, being your guinea pig."

Betty leaned in and lowered her voice. "We've bought the empty store next door and we're going to expand."

"Hey, that's wonderful. What are you thinking? More booths? Tables?"

"The Sunrise Bakery." She straightened, a grin brightening her face.

Angelique placed her hand over her heart. "I'm in heaven. Aunt Rebecca is going to love hearing this."

Betty winked. "It was actually talking with Rebecca that sealed it for me. She'll be my head baker. And we're going to carry local products like jams and jellies, wines from the area." She looked from woman to woman. "We kept it under wraps until Jerry was back on his feet and the papers were signed."

Aimee had a far-off look in her eye. "There used to be a bakery down the block from where we lived. Mom would let my sister and me ride our bikes down there on Saturday morning to get fresh *kolaches* right out of the oven." She closed her eyes. "I can still smell that scent. Is that weird?" She glanced up at Betty. "This town could really use a bakery."

"We haven't worked out all the details yet." She looked at Liberty. "But we were hoping, if you're ready, and since you did such a nice job with redecorating the café, that maybe you'd consider helping design the bakery as well?"

Liberty's face lit up. "It would be my pleasure, Betty. Truly a pleasure. Thank you for thinking of me."

"Perfect. I'll let Jerry know and we can set up a time to visit with you to discuss ideas." Betty smiled at the women. "I love the lot of you, you know that, right?"

"We love you, too, Betty," Sally said. "But I'd love you more if you could whip me up one of your famous gourmet grilled cheese sandwiches on sourdough... the ones with the thin pear slices and bacon?"

"Yum, that sounds good, with a cup of tomato bisque?" Angelique added.

Aimee licked her lips. "That sounds delish. Make that three with soup. And that still leaves room for dessert."

"Coming right up, ladies. How about you, Miss Liberty?" Betty asked.

"Just soup and crackers, please. Then bring on the desserts." She waggled her fingers.

After Betty left, Liberty nudged Sally. "So, we've all been waiting to hear how your bachelor date with Mr. Saunders went? Pretty good, I'm guessing by the sound of things?"

They looked at Sally and she felt her cheeks growing warm. "Aw, come on now, you know I'm not the kiss and tell type."

Liberty raised her brows. "I see. Kissing was involved. Interesting." Her dark eyes glittered with mischief and while it was great to see Liberty back to her ornery self, Sally wasn't sure she appreciated the attention on her. "Rein mentioned that Clay hasn't stopped smiling for the past three days that they've worked together."

"I did hear that his truck was seen parked on your street the other morning," Aimee teased.

Sally held up her hands in surrender. "Okay, okay, as if you all don't already know, yes, we are officially 'seeing' each other."

Liberty grinned. "Apparently seeing *a lot* of each other from what I hear."

"We know you're seeing each other. Angelique chimed in. "We're just curious if, you know... you're happy."

"By happy, we mean, does the man rise to the occasion?" Liberty goaded with a wicked smile.

Sally looked aghast at Aimee. "Do I ask personal questions about your sex lives?"

Aimee shrugged. "I live under a rock, don't look at me."

Liberty pointed a finger at her. "Under a rock is not how you got pregnant again, my dear. Though hard-as-a rock comes to mind."

"You're wicked," Aimee responded with a grin. "But I like that about you." She held up her water glass to toast her sister-in-law.

Angelique giggled, then gasped, and straightened in her seat. The table fell silent.

"Are you okay?" Aimee lay her hand on Angelique's shoulder.

"The baby kicked." She blinked. "He kicked." Her eyes welled.

Liberty leaned over the table and pressed her hand to Angelique's belly. "Let me feel."

Sally glanced at Aimee and saw she was no better at holding in the tears as they watched Liberty's fascination.

Liberty's eyes widened. A fat tear plopped on her cheek. "I felt him. Is that a foot? That's amazing. I never got to feel that." Her chin quivered as she sat back in her seat.

Sally put her arm around Liberty and hugged her. "You will."

"Yeah?" Liberty sniffed and forced a smile.

"I have no doubt," Sally said, hugging the woman again. She looked at Aimee, who regarded her with a steady gaze. Sally smiled.

Her friend blinked and her gaze narrowed. "Sally?"

Sally swallowed. She'd hoped she could keep her secret to herself until at least she'd had time to go to the doctor for confirmation. Given how she'd been feeling, she'd gone ahead and done an early home kit and discovered the news just after Clay left for California. She hadn't had the chance to even tell him yet.

Angelique looked from Aimee to Sally. "What?"

"You're pregnant," Aimee stated quietly, holding Sally's gaze.

Liberty let out a yelp and hugged Sally.

"Ladies, can you tone it down, I'm trying to hear the news."

Betty's reprimand quieted the celebration and all eyes followed hers to the television that hung on the wall behind the counter.

The national news was showing footage of a standoff between police and a man holding a man, woman, and two children hostage in a Sacramento home. "Police indicate he's wounded one," said a reporter. "The man inside, whose name has not been released, has threatened to take the lives of everyone, including himself. One officer tells us that the crisis began about mid-afternoon and about thirty minutes ago, two young boys were released."

They went to a previously recorded clip of two young boys running across a front yard into the arms of awaiting law enforcement.

Everyone turned to Sally. They were Clay's nephews.

"The man inside holding these people hostage has a violent temper. He's unpredictable." If anyone on earth understood unpredictable temper, it was Clay. He brushed his hand over his mouth, his patience wearing thin with the officer who he reminded himself a dozen times, was just doing his job.

"Yes, we understand, Mr. Saunders. If you could tell us as much of what you remember—how you got here, anything your sister might have said that could help us."

Clay stood with an officer hidden behind the small moving truck he'd parked in the drive. He'd seen the rental car, but not seen Louis's, which was in the garage. It wasn't until he'd dodged a spray of bullets from the front window that he realized something was wrong. That's when he called the police. "My sister, Julie, called me last night. She was frightened and asked me to come out and help her and the kids—my two nephews—out of the house. She said her husband had become more abusive, more violent recently."

"Had she mentioned ever calling the police before today?"

Clay shook his head, doubting Julie would have attempted it, more out of fear of repercussion than anything. "I don't know, she never said."

"Are you aware if he owns a gun?" the officer asked.

Clay eyed the man. "He shot several rounds at me. My guess is yes."

The officer patiently nodded. "What I meant by that is that had she ever mentioned him threatening her or anyone before with a gun?"

Clay blew out a breath. He wanted to do something. He felt helpless and helpless wasn't one of his favorite things to be. "Not that I'm aware of. His weapon of choice with my sister was his fist." Clay looked over the man's shoulder and searched the side of the house, trying to remember if there were any windows that led to the family room in the basement. "Look, what can we do here? My friend and my sister—those boys' mother—is still in there with that nut job."

"Your friend? That would be 'Hank' that you mentioned earlier." The officer flipped back through his notes.

Clay realized they were trying to establish a timeline, leaving no stone unturned. If it would put this ass away for a long time, he'd try to remember

Julie's dress size if necessary. "I got to the Billings airport hoping to get on stand-by. That's where I ran into Hank Richardson, an old friend since…" Clay paused, doing the math. "Since college. He'd just landed, was coming in for a surprise visit. I told him the situation, and he offered to help me out. As soon as he gassed up, we took off and flew into Sacramento International. We rented a car and drove straight to the rental place to pick up the truck my sister had reserved by phone."

Clay rubbed his forehead. He'd kicked himself a million times since agreeing to Hank's proposal. "Hank offered to go on ahead and help my sister stage the boxes for loading."

"Was there ever anything between Mr. Richardson and your sister?"

Clay looked at the man like he was daft, but his memory triggered back to the auction and the comment Hank had made. "Nothing even remotely recent. A crush, a very long time ago. Nothing since." He didn't add, *that I'm aware of.*

The officer spoke into the walkie-talkie attached to his shoulder. "Two hostages. Probable domestic violence situation. Possible third party involved. Relative of a female hostage indicates a past violent nature from the suspect, believed to be her husband. Apparently came home to find she was leaving him." He glanced at Clay for verification of what he'd relayed.

Clay nodded. "Is there anything I can do? Talk to him, maybe?"

"Do you think he'd listen to you. Mr. Saunders?" the officer asked.

Given that Louis chose bullets instead of a handshake made Clay think no. He saw a gray truck stop down the block and watched as several men dressed in special gear began to fan out in the neighborhood. Television crews had been kept behind a police barricade two blocks away. It occurred to him that they were bringing in a SWAT team in the event that negotiation efforts might fail. The longer they waited, the higher the risk for all involved. They'd likely use tear gas. There might be collateral damage. He couldn't stand by and watch this play out.

The officer focused on speaking to another never saw Clay slip away, ducking low as he ran along the side of the house. He knew the layout. He'd gone over everything in his mind and deduced that they were likely in the front room. Given the number of shots fired—up to ten if his memory served, and most into the side of the truck—he guessed probably a universal gun, used for home security, likely a Glock 19. If so, that meant he had roughly five rounds left at the most—less, if he'd used any before Clay arrived. He put that thought aside as he rounded the back corner of the house, delighted to see that the sliding glass door to the deck was open. *Thank you, Julie for your obsession with fresh air.* Clay crawled under the railing and inched his way to standing beside the door. He heard Julie inside, pleading with Louis and his heart twisted with fear.

"Louis, you need to let me get this man some help. He's bleeding."

Clay noted one of the SWAT team circling behind the house next door. He held up his hand, identifying himself as friendly.

"Louis, please, you don't have to do this. We can sit down and talk this out."

"Talk? You were planning to take the boys away from me, Julie. I can't… I won't let you do that."

"They won't have either of us, Louis, if you hurt me. There'll be no one to care for them."

"Not even that gimp brother of yours?"

Clay had had about as much as he could handle. He spied the team member signaling to another man. In their hands, a black object—likely tear gas.

"Clay is a good man, Louis," Julie said.

"And I'm not, is that it?" he demanded. "And who is this guy? Is he a good man, too, Julie?"

"I didn't say you weren't a good man, Louis. I didn't mean that." Weariness laced her voice.

Praying the kitchen wall would serve as cover, he peeked around the curtain and saw Louis with his back turned. Quietly lifting the screen off the frame, he slipped inside and ducked down behind the kitchen island. He saw Hank slumped against the wall. Blood soaked one shoulder. His skin was pasty, had a sheen. That wasn't good.

"What's going on out there? It's too quiet," Louis said as he hid behind the front curtain and eased it back with the gun.

Seizing what he felt might be his only chance, Clay sprung forward and tackled the man from behind. The gun slipped from his hand and slid across the floor. He held the struggling man in a firm chokehold. "Julie, yell to them it's safe. The suspect is secured."

She complied and soon after several officers stormed through the front door.

Clay stood to relinquish his hold on Louis, holding his hardened gaze as they led him away.

"That was brave, Mr. Saunders. Stupid, but brave." The officer who'd interviewed him eyed him. "Army, I'm guessing." He smiled then. "I'll find a way to dismiss interfering in police procedure."

"Thanks," Clay said, and shook his hand.

A medical team had Hank on a gurney wheeling him out of the house. He looked up as Clay walked up next to him and took his hand. "You're going to be okay."

Hank gave him a weary grin. "Just do me a favor."

"You got it." Clay leaned down to hear him.

"Don't ever ask me to help you move again."

Clay squeezed Hank's hand and got from the team where they were taking him. The bullet had gone through clean, missing the bone. He'd lost a lot of blood, but he'd fully recover. He went back inside to where Julie was talking to officers.

She rose to greet him, putting her arms around his waist, she buried her face in his shirt. "It's over, Julie. You and the boys are safe."

He nudged her to look out the window and she ran out the front door meeting the two boys on the front lawn. Dropping to her knees, she embraced them. Only one thought entered his mind as he watched them—

God, he missed Sally.

Realizing how long it'd had been since his last communication he pulled out his phone to see the number of missed calls and texts that she'd left him.

If she'd seen any of this on the news, she must be in a world of worry.

He checked the time and knew she'd be getting ready for bed about now. God, how he wanted to be there. He dialed her number, his heart at peace when she answered.

"Clay?"

"It's me, I'm so sorry. My phone was turned low and, well, it's been a little nuts out here."

"Are you all right? I saw the news. There was a gurney—"

"That was Hank."

"Hank? Hank Richardson?"

"Long story, Sally. God, it's good to hear your voice. I have definitely missed you."

"You're not hurt?"

"I'm good… fine."

"Julie, the boys?" she asked.

"All safe, doing fine."

"Well… *I'm* not fine," she blurted hysterically.

"I know, baby. I know. It's all over now and I'm looking forward to getting back to life in that sleepy town. That's not true—I'm just looking forward to holding you while you sleep. Have I mentioned that I love you?" He heard her swallow. "Just a couple of days, okay?"

"Okay. Drive safely." There was a pause, as though she had more to say. Concerned that she wasn't sure of how to tell him what was on her mind, he nudged her a bit. "Sally, is everything okay?" His heart thudded in his chest. She hadn't responded with similar endearments. The past crept up and taunted his brain.

"Everything is good, Clay. I'm so relieved to hear you're okay and no one was hurt badly. I just miss you. Please, drive safely. Let me know if you're stopping. I miss you like crazy. Does that sound silly?"

Clay smiled. "It sounds like heaven to me, sweetheart. I'll be home soon."

Home. Clay thought about it on the drive back to Montana, about how effortlessly the word had rolled off his tongue. Now, within a few miles of the turn-off to the ranch, the reality settled peacefully in his heart. It was just after four o'clock. Barring any unforeseen issues at school, he hoped to find Sally waiting at the ranch. Seeing his turnoff—a new metal arch that spanned the entrance with the new logo of a horse head and the words 'Last Hope Ranch'—he flipped his signal on to alert Julie, behind him in a rental car, to follow.

Hank had been kept an extra day at the hospital and was to be released for flying tomorrow. He intended to fly into Billings in the next couple of days just to check in on everyone. Clay knew that Hank's real concern was for Julie.

She'd hired a lawyer before they left and filed for divorce. She wanted nothing from him, with the exception of child support. Her lawyer, while trying to suggest otherwise, finally told Julie she would handle everything and would be in touch. Julie wasn't sure of her plans yet, but she was determined to make a better life for her and the boys.

Clay guided the truck down the asphalt drive, past the main house, and pulled in near the entrance of the two-bedroom cabin just a few doors up from his cabin. He climbed from the cab, stretched his arms and raised his brows as he saw the Kinnison clan—including Michael and Rebecca—coming out of the cabin.

"Hey guys," he called out.

Sally ran into his arms and hugged his neck.

"I'm so glad to be home," he said, pressing his face into the warm curve of her neck. He couldn't remember a time in years when those words truly made me happy.

"Listen," Aimee said, walking toward Julie. "We've got supper up at the main house, thanks to Rebecca and Betty, who sent down some casseroles that we just put in your freezer." Aimee put her arm around Julie's shoulder. "It's been a long drive. "Let's go get a glass of wine and relax while supper is finishing up. These guys can unload the truck."

Julie looked over her shoulder at Clay as she walked up the path surrounded by women of the Kinnison ranch. Emilee and the boys wasted no time scrambling to sit on the fence and watch the horses grazing in the corral.

"Five minutes, Em," Dalton called to her, "then you all go get washed up for dinner."

"Yes, sir," she responded.

Rein slapped Clay on the shoulder, then pulled him in for a hug. "Heard about what you did out there. Course, it was Hank's 'version'. You should probably enlighten me. Why don't you guys go on up to the house. We've got this."

Clay tugged Sally's hand as they approached the back of the barn. "Do you mind if we take a detour through the barn? There's something about—"

"The smell, right?" Sally interjected. "I've always loved how—"

"Peaceful it feels," Clay finished. They walked hand-in-hand through the barn, the gentle sounds of the horses greeting them. "I missed these guys about as much as I missed you."

"Understandable."

He led her to the old storage box where he'd first kissed her. It seemed like a million years ago and just yesterday—it puzzled him. But how he felt about Sally... that was forever. "Remember this place?" He rubbed his thumb over the back of her hand.

"I do. It's where you first kissed me," Sally said.

"Wait, I kissed you?" He frowned. "I seem to remember it being the other way around."

Sally eyed him with a smile. "Your kiss was much better, as I recall."

"Yeah?" Clay tipped her chin to meet his eyes.

"I liked it... a lot."

"Me, too," he said quietly before brushing his lips to hers. Like heaven on earth, her lips parted to greet him in the way he'd been dreaming of for days. "It'd probably be rude to skip supper, wouldn't it?"

She skimmed her hand over the front of his shirt and licked her lips. "People would probably notice."

That prompted another kiss. "Hey, Sally?"

"Yes?" Her voice had that sleepy, sexy tone he loved more than air.

"I think it's time we took our relationship to the next level."

She playfully bit his lip causing him to groan with pure pleasure. "I think we've already done that."

"I want my nephews to be able to call you Aunt Sally."

She leaned back and searched his face. "Wait, are you suggesting that it's not enough we have—what was it—off the charts sex?"

Clay thought a moment, then nodded, "Yeah, that's it. Crazy as it sounds. It's not enough. You love me, I love you. Hell, the other night I pulled up to your house and just sat there watching you through the kitchen window."

"That's a little creepy, to be honest." She smiled.

"It made me realize that's what I want."

"To watch me in the kitchen every night?" She made a face.

"Sally, sometimes—you make me crazy."

Sally held his face and kissed him gently. "Sweetheart, I do understand what you're saying. There's nothing that would turn me on more than to come home and watch you cooking in the kitchen. Does that help?"

He grinned. "I can do that."

"Of course, and trust me, you will or we'll likely starve." She kissed him again. "Oh, just one more thing. As long as we're throwing around labels like aunt and uncle, how do you feel about *daddy?*

EPILOGUE

"Did you hear that Kaylee moved in with Tyler Janzen?" Angelique told Sally at breakfast two months later. "I swear he has picked up every stray in a fifty- mile radius just as an excuse to drop by the shelter."

"*Twitter pated*," Sally said with a grin, then looked at Angelique. "My dad used to say people and animals got *twitter pated* in the spring. I think it's a reference to *Bambi or Thumper*—one of those." Spring had indeed come in earnest to End of the Line. Sally welcomed the gentle rains that seemed to turn the world from a dull brown to a vibrant green overnight. She welcomed getting past a rugged bout of morning sickness and had managed—merely out of curiosity—to seek Emilee's intuition, but only received a 'it's a girl or a boy' from the gifted, but precocious youngster.

The demolition going on next door with the bakery renovations made talking a bit more of a challenge at the café these days.

Hank, his arm still in a sling, opened the café door for Julie, only to have her boys rush through to find a seat. "Hey, you two, back here and let's try that again," he said with a smile.

"Interesting," Angelique commented as she slathered honey on her fresh biscuit.

Sally watched as the two boys ambled back outside and held the door for their mom, who hugged them immediately. It had appeared that End of the Line and a few weeks at the Last Hope Ranch had solidified Julies plans to stick around.

"Hey, Sally," Julie leaned down to hug her. "Hi, Angelique. We came up to look at a vacant apartment upstairs. Betty thought it'd be great for me and the boys."

Sally grinned. "I'm glad you've decided to stay."

"The boys absolutely love it here." She sighed. "The wide open spaces. Fresh air. And never mind Michael taking them on trail rides."

"It's a great place to raise kids, no doubt there," Angelique offered.

"Okay, I'm ready, you guys want to see this apartment?" Betty stepped from the kitchen. "Look here, boys. These are *kolaches*. Sink your teeth into one of these, if it's okay with mom."

The pair looked at their mom, and received a nod.

"Come on, then." Betty ushered them through a door behind the counter that led one way up the stairs to the apartment.

"You don't happen to have another one of those?" Hank asked, sticking his head inside the kitchen.

"Help yourself," Betty called. "New recipe. Testing it out."

Hank grabbed a pastry and saluted Sally with it as he tagged behind.

"Looks like the population of End of the Line is about to increase by three," Angelique said with a raised brow. She glanced at her belly and then Sally's slight protrusion. "At least in the interim."

Clay appeared from the kitchen where they'd busted a back entrance to the bakery. He was covered from head-to-toe with a fine layer of dirt and dust. Emphasis on *fine*. Sally couldn't believe she woke up to that every morning.

"Hey, honey. I just ran into Hank and I guess he's going to be around for a few days, so I thought I'd invite him to supper. He'll be staying down at the cabins, but honey, he's a worse cook than you. Do you mind?"

"Why, thank you, my love. Of course, I don't mind. By the way, what are we having for dinner tonight?"

He shrugged. "I don't know. Surprise me. Take something out of the freezer. I'll take it from there." He bent down and kissed her soundly. "Thanks. Love you," he said as he walked away.

"Love you more," Sally called back.

"Do you think he'd give Dalton cooking classes?" Angelique asked. "And news flash—Hank is sticking around a few days? Hum... population heading up by one more, you think?"

Sally smiled. She decided to wait awhile before breaking the news about her last ultrasound visit.

DEAR READERS

I hope you enjoyed returning to End of the Line, Montana and seeing how Clay and Sally managed, with the help and support of friends and family, to realize that sometimes what your heart is searching for is standing right in front of you. There are so many more stories needing to be told from End of the Line. Starting with the Kinnison Legacy trilogy (Rugged Hearts, Rustler's Heart, and Renegade Hearts) you can visit End of the Line and meet its wonderful, quirky residents! Would love to hear from you about whose story you'd like to see in the new series—The Last Hope Ranch. Email me at: amandamcintyre.author@gmail.com

And down the road, a wonderful charitable project I'm really excited about! Coming soon- Betty's Sunrise Café Cookbook!! To celebrate, I'm sharing with you, Betty's NO PEEK STEW recipe and a quick and yummy BEER BREAD recipe that goes divinely with it!!

Read the books that inspired the
Last Hope Ranch series!

RUGGED HEARTS
RUSTLER'S HEART
RENEGADE HEART

More at amazon.com/author/amandamcintyre

NO PEEK STEW

In large oven-ready pot:
1.5 pounds of stew meat (beef ribs, cut in bite-size pieces also works)
1 yellow onion (chopped)
*3-4 washed potatoes (cut in chunks)
*3 stalks celery (cut in chunks)
*1 cup tomato juice
*1 teaspoon sugar
*2 tablespoons tapioca
*1 pound carrots (cut in chunks)
* Salt and pepper to taste.
Put lid on. Bake in oven @250* for 5 hours. Do NOT peek!

BEER BREAD

Grease Loaf pan.
Bake in 400* oven 40 minutes
Mix; 3 cups self-rising flour*1/2 cup white sugar *
1 can beer

OTHER BOOKS BY AMANDA MCINTYRE YOU MIGHT BE INTERESTED IN:

Contemporary Romance:
No Strings Attached, Book I (Last Hope Ranch)
Rugged Hearts, Book I (Kinnison Legacy)
Rustler's Heart, Book II (Kinnison Legacy
Renegade Hearts, Book III (Kinnison Legacy)
Stranger in Paradise
Tides of Autumn
Unfinished Dreams
Wish You Were Here
Historical Erotic Thriller:
The Dark Seduction of Miss Jane
Historical/Erotic Romance:
The Master & the Muses *
The Diary of Cozette *
Tortured *
The Pleasure Garden *
Winter's Desire *
Dark Pleasures *
Starred titles available in audio and international languages
Contemporary Adult Fiction:
Private Party
Mirror, Mirror
Naughty Bits, Vol III
Historical time-travel:
Closer To You (Previously Wild & Unruly)
Para/Fantasy:
Tirnan 'Oge

ABOUT THE AUTHOR

Amanda McIntyre's passion is telling character-driven stories with a penchant for placing ordinary people placed in extraordinary situations. A bestselling author, her work is published internationally in print, E-book, and audio.

She writes sizzling contemporary and hot historical romance and believes no matter what, love will find a way.

~*~

Connect with Amanda:

WEBSITE:
http://www.amandamcintyresbooks.com/
FACEBOOK:
https://www.facebook.com/AmandaMcIntyreAutho
rFanPage
TWITTER:
https://twitter.com/amandamcintyre1
GOODREADS:
https://www.goodreads.com/author/show/519786.A
manda_McIntyre
AMAZON AUTHOR(find all my books here)
http://www.amazon.com/-/e/B002C1KH2Q
NEWSLETTER:
http://madmimi.com/signups/110714/join